PUFFIN BOOKS

The Victory Dogs

Megan Rix lives with her husband by a river in England. When she's not writing she can be found walking her two golden retrievers, Traffy and Bella, who are often in the river.

D1344889

Books by Megan Rix

THE GREAT ESCAPE
THE VICTORY DOGS
THE BOMBER DOG

The Victory Dogs

megan rix

PUFFIN

PUFFIN BOOKS

Published by the Penguin Group
Penguin Books Ltd, 80 Strand, London WC2R 0RL, England
Penguin Group (USA) Inc., 375 Hudson Street, New York, New York 10014, USA
Penguin Group (Canada), 90 Eglinton Avenue East, Suite 700, Toronto, Ontario, Canada M4P 2Y3
(a division of Pearson Penguin Canada Inc.)
Penguin Ireland, 25 St Stephen's Green, Dublin 2, Ireland (a division of Penguin Books Ltd)
Penguin Group (Australia), 707 Collins Street, Melbourne, Victoria 3008, Australia
(a division of Pearson Australia Group Pty Ltd)
Penguin Books India Pvt Ltd, 11 Community Centre, Panchsheel Park, New Delhi – 110 017, India
Penguin Group (NZ), 67 Apollo Drive, Rosedale, Auckland 0632, New Zealand
(a division of Pearson New Zealand Ltd)
Penguin Books (South Africa) (Pty) Ltd, Block D, Rosebank Office Park, 181 Jan Smuts Avenue, Parktown
North, Gauteng 2193, South Africa

Penguin Books Ltd, Registered Offices: 80 Strand, London WC2R 0R, England

puffinbooks.com

First published 2013

003

Text copyright © Megan Rix, 2013
Map © TfL from the London Transport Museum collection
Chapter illustrations copyright © Puffin Books, 2013
All rights reserved

The moral right of the author has been asserted
This book is a work of fiction. Names, characters, places and incidents are either the product of the
author's imagination or are used fictitiously, and any resemblance to actual persons, living or dead, business
establishments, events or locales is entirely coincidental.

Set in 13/16 pt Baskerville. Typeset by Palimpsest Book Production Ltd, Falkirk, Stirlingshire
Printed and bound in Great Britain by Clays Ltd, Elcograf S.p.A.

British Library Cataloguing in Publication Data
A CIP catalogue record for this book is available from the British Library

ISBN: 978-0-241-41510-8

www.greenpenguin.co.uk

MIX
Paper from
responsible sources
FSC® C018179
www.fsc.org

Penguin Books is committed to a sustainable
future for our business, our readers and our planet.
This book is made from Forest Stewardship
Council™ certified paper.

In memory of the heroes of the Second World War —
both two-legged and four.

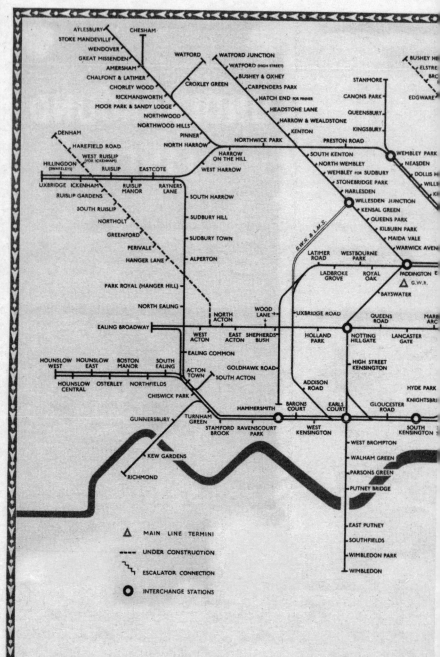

© TfL from the London Transport Museum collection

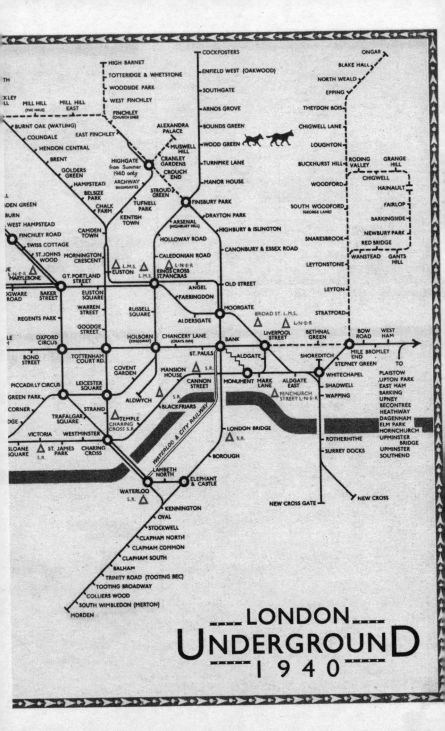

LONDON
UNDERGROUND
1940

Chapter 1

London, 1940

Misty had a bed of her own, by the fire downstairs, but she always chose to lie on Jack's bed. The soft, cream-coated dog with floppy ears yawned and stretched her large pregnant tummy out across the bed and watched as her beloved owner twisted the green woollen tie round his neck and then undid it again with a loud sigh.

Twelve-year-old Amy watched her older brother too.

'Can I help?' she asked him.

But Jack shook his head. He'd have to manage it by himself once he was in the army.

'Why do things like tying ties and shoelaces have to be so tricky?' he said.

Misty gave a soft whine as if she were agreeing with him.

Amy stroked Misty's furry head and began

reciting the rhyme they'd been taught at school to help them remember how to knot their ties:

> '*The hare sees the fox and hops over the log, under the log, around the log once . . . around the log twice . . . and dives into his hole . . . safe and sound.*'

Jack grinned and finally managed to get the tie tied. But no sooner had he done so than Misty started scratching frantically at the brown candlewick bedspread, tearing at it with her paws and biting at it with her teeth.

'Misty, no!' said Jack.

Misty stopped, mid-scratch, and looked over at him, her soft brown eyes staring straight into his.

She'd been acting very oddly over the past few days – crying and hiding in corners and under the kitchen dresser, ripping Jack and Amy's father's newspaper to shreds before he'd even had a chance to read it. She'd already pulled the bedspread off Jack's bed twice and bundled it up on the floor.

Destructive behaviour like this wasn't like Misty at all. Ever since she'd been a puppy she had been a steady, gentle sort of dog.

At first, they'd thought that somehow she knew Jack was going away and this was her way of saying she wanted him to stay. But then they'd realized that Misty was in fact pregnant. Once they knew that, her behaviour seemed perfectly natural – they just had to remind her not to act like that indoors!

'She's trying to make a nest again!' said Amy. 'To find somewhere safe for her puppies to be born.'

'Good girl, Misty,' Jack said. 'You're all right.'

He sat down on the bed beside the dog his mother and father had finally got him, after years of begging, six years ago. A black-and-white photo of Misty was on the cabinet next to his bed all ready for him to pack and take with him.

This was going to be Misty's first litter of puppies and Jack was gutted that he was going to miss it.

'If only I could be here with her,' he said for the hundredth time.

But they both knew he couldn't be. Jack was eighteen and had had his call-up papers to join the army. His orders were to report to the basic training camp first thing in the morning to fulfil his military service duty. After that, he'd be going to the front. There was no way out of it.

'It's Jack who should be all jittery, not you,' Amy told Misty as Jack pulled at the green woollen tie that was half strangling him. 'He's the one going off to war. All you're going to be doing is having pups – and that'll be lovely.'

Misty pressed herself close to Jack and then crawled on to his lap as if she were still a young puppy. He could feel her heart racing. He kissed the top of Misty's furry head. He was going to miss her so badly. She'd slept on his bed every night for the past six years, ever since she'd come to live with them as a ten-week-old puppy. He didn't know how he was going to sleep without her there.

Misty stretched up her neck so Jack could scratch under her chin.

'Promise you'll take good care of her?' he said to Amy.

'I promise,' she said. 'Two walks a day and all the treats I'm allowed to give her. She can sleep in my room if she likes, but I bet she'll keep sleeping in your room as usual, waiting on your bed for you to come home.'

Jack's leaving was probably going to be hardest for Misty. She couldn't be expected to understand where he'd gone or why he had to go. All she'd know was that he'd left her.

'Make sure you give her lots of strokes,' said Jack.

Amy smiled. She knew how much Jack loved Misty and what an important task he was entrusting to her.

'At least a thousand strokes a day,' she said.

Amy couldn't imagine what the house was going to be like without Jack there. But she was sure it would be a sadder, lonelier place without him. He was six years older than her and some big brothers might not have liked their little sister tagging along with them all the time. But Jack wasn't like that. He was the best big brother in the world.

Amy swallowed down the lump in her throat. Now was not the time for crying. She had to be strong for Jack and Misty, and told herself she wasn't the only one having to say goodbye. Amy knew that hundreds of people up and down the country were saying goodbye to the people they loved as more and more men and boys were called up. They too would be frightened and worried about when they'd see each other again.

At first, the war had felt very far away from Amy's world, but no one doubted England was truly at war now. At school they were growing vegetables on the playing field and knitting scarves and socks to keep the soldiers warm. But Amy wished there was something more she could do to help with the war effort. Anything for it to be over with as soon as possible.

'I'm glad she has you,' Jack said as he stroked Misty.

He stood up and pushed his arms into the suit jacket. Then he laced up the shoes he'd polished so hard he could see his reflection in them.

'Ready to show Mum and Dad?' he said. Jack was trying on his dad's suit to wear the next morning – it felt a bit like getting ready for the first day of school.

Misty jumped awkwardly off the bed and followed Jack and Amy as they went down the stairs.

The front door was open and there was a bucket

beside it. Once a week, regular as clockwork, their mother, Mrs Dolan, cleaned the front doorstep until it shone. Most of their neighbours did the same. Mrs Dolan stood up as soon as she saw Jack.

'Oh, son,' she said, her voice breaking at the sight of her boy going off to war in his father's best suit. She clenched her floral apron tightly in her fist to stop herself from welling up. 'Your father will be so proud.'

Doorstep forgotten and cleaning materials abandoned, she led Jack to the front room where his father was waiting. This room had their best furniture and ornaments in it and was reserved for visitors and special occasions. There was a black upright piano in the corner, a floral patterned sofa, two armchairs and a print of a seascape on the wall. Mrs Dolan closed the door so Misty couldn't follow them inside as she was never allowed in the sitting room.

'Here he is, all grown up,' Mrs Dolan said as her unbidden tears turned to sobs. 'And going off to fight.'

'Hush, mother,' Mr Dolan told her, and she sniffed and wiped her tears away on her apron. 'Our boy needs you to be strong.'

Mrs Dolan nodded, not trusting herself to speak. Amy took her mother's hand and squeezed it gently.

Misty stared at the closed sitting-room door for a moment and then padded along the hallway to the open front door and sniffed. There was a lazy late Saturday afternoon feeling in the soft, warm air. She didn't attempt to go out. She'd never been tempted to stray although there'd been opportunities aplenty in the past, but the air with its myriad smells from the street was too interesting not to sniff. Next-door's dog, over-the-road's cat, the three round metal pig bins by the lamp post all made her sensitive nose twitch.

She watched as a boy emptied the scraps from his family's breakfast and Saturday lunch into one of them, waving his hand to ward off the host of bluebottles that buzzed round him.

Every few days the bins were collected and sent to local farms where they were emptied into the pigs' troughs before being returned and quickly filled up again.

Misty stepped out on to the front-garden path and sniffed. But then she heard a strange sound, little more than a hum, like a soft insect drone at first. Too quiet for a human ear to detect, but Misty heard it. It grew louder and louder. Misty hurried to the closed door of the sitting room and whined softly.

Inside the room Amy was the first to hear the distant but steady drone.

'What's that noise?' she asked.

The sound was strangely ominous and her parents looked at each other uneasily.

'What is it?' she repeated, her voice now fearful as the noise grew ever louder.

'Plane engines!' said Jack.

Outside in the hallway Misty whined and scratched at the door more frantically. Then came the sound of the siren, wailing faintly at first, but soon growing louder and louder until it was deafening. In a panic, Misty ran from the hallway, out of the house and down the front path and along the street, on and on, desperate to get away from the dreadful wailing that filled her head, thinking only of protecting her unborn pups.

As the air-raid siren joined the sound of the planes, Mr Dolan grabbed his wife's hand. They'd been warned that there could be bombs at any time, but were not expecting them just before teatime on a warm September afternoon.

'Bombs!' he shouted. 'Out to the shelter, quickly!'

The four of them ran from the sitting room through the kitchen door and out into the back garden, past the outside toilet, to the Anderson shelter at the rear. Mr Dolan pulled away the sacking he'd used to cover the small opening and helped his wife and daughter down the shortened ladder.

'In you go.'

'Misty!' Jack shouted. He turned back to fetch her, but his father grabbed his arm firmly and wouldn't let go when Jack tried to pull away.

'No, son, you can't go back. She'll be fine,' he said and he dragged Jack into the shelter, holding his arm so tightly his fingers pinched into his son's flesh.

'But . . .'

'You stay,' Mr Dolan insisted.

Inside the shelter they huddled together as other sirens joined the first, wailing their terrible warning. Jack and Amy fretted about Misty and longed for the all-clear to sound, but they didn't try to go out before it did. In the distance they could hear people screaming and the sound of the planes, followed by a piercing whistling as they dropped their bombs.

Amy's mum clasped Amy to her as a bomb exploded somewhere in the distance, but still near enough to make the earth shake and their ears ring with its horrible, dreadful, ear-wrenching loudness. Inside the Anderson shelter it was dark, but outside the sun still shone. They all instinctively shielded their heads with their hands as more bombs followed the first; they seemed to be exploding all around them. Shrapnel and debris showered down on the top of the shelter for what felt like hours.

Misty ran through the North London streets like a wild thing, heart racing, with no sense or care as to where she was going, until finally she slowed down and could run no more. She was six years old, the equivalent of middle-aged in human years, and no puppy any more.

She panted with exhaustion as, long after it had first started, the sirens' wailing finally stopped. But the panic around her didn't. People ran this way and that, stumbled and fell, lost shoes and sometimes stopped to pick them up, but more often left them abandoned, not daring to delay.

No one had any time to pay attention to Misty or even notice that she was lost and alone. They were too busy running for safety themselves to hear her whimpering or see her trembling.

Misty wasn't as confident as some dogs. She'd always been more hesitant, reserved, and, although she loved to be stroked, she wouldn't push herself forward unless she was sure of her welcome – even within her own family. So she didn't approach any of the passing strangers.

One woman, wearing a bottle-green scarf, half stopped, but she was pulled away by her friend.

'The very least you'll get is fleas.'

'Poor thing – doesn't look like a stray. I can see its registration disc.'

Misty took a hopeful step towards them and the woman who said she had fleas waved her handbag at her.

'Go on, scat!'

Misty immediately backed off. Head down, she padded on aimlessly, quite lost for the first time in her life. And now she had more than just herself to worry about. There were the puppies that had been growing inside her for the past two months. She could feel them moving. What's more, she knew instinctively that they were almost ready to be born.

Someone ran past her saying, 'Not today, not today, not today,' over and over. London had been warned about the bombings for so long, no one could quite believe it was actually happening now.

'Three hundred planes . . .'

'I heard more . . .'

'Bombs . . .'

'Targeting the South London docks . . .' said the passing voices.

Tentatively Misty approached a passer-by dragging a dog by its lead, but she backed away quickly when the owner yelled at her.

'Get away!'

Soon the sirens' wail started again and more people rushed past Misty. She started to run again too, although her paws ached and she was heavy with the pups. All she really wanted to do was lie down and sleep.

Chapter 2

On and on, bomb after bomb, it continued until Amy thought it would never stop; but finally it did.

It was just after six in the evening when the all-clear siren sounded. Jack and Amy scrambled out of the Anderson shelter and ran back to the house to check on Misty. Mrs Dolan gasped in horror when she saw their house: all the windows had been shattered.

'At least it's still standing,' Mr Dolan said, putting his arm round her shoulders. 'I'll have them boarded up in no time.'

'We could have been . . . in there.'

'But we weren't.'

He opened the back door and Mrs Dolan gasped again.

'My kitchen!' she said. Cups and plates were smashed as was the glass door of her cupboard. Chairs were flung across the room and there was dust and dirt everywhere.

'At least the house didn't take a direct hit,' Mr

Dolan said, gritting his teeth and thinking of the neighbouring houses that had not been so lucky.

'My best plates . . . the dust . . .' Mrs Dolan whispered as she looked around at the damage.

'What's that funny smell?' Amy asked. 'Like cabbage . . .'

'Gas!' said Mr Dolan and he ran to turn it off at the mains. 'I'm going to warn the neighbours – it could catch fire or even cause another explosion.'

'Misty! Misty!' cried Jack as he ran from room to room.

'Here, girl!' Amy called out as she followed him. Her stomach twisted as she dreaded finding Misty horribly injured or dead. If only they'd been able to take her with them. She'd have been safe in the shelter. How could they have left her behind?

'Misty?' Amy said as she opened the door to her room. Just like downstairs there was plaster everywhere. Her books were all over the floor and the glass in her windows had been smashed.

'Oh no,' she said when she saw the photograph of her grandmother and grandfather lying shattered on the floor. More glass fell out of the frame as she picked it up.

'Careful, Amy,' her mother said when she saw what she was doing.

'My picture of Gran and Grandpa . . .' said Amy helplessly and Mrs Dolan hugged her.

Amy's softly spoken grandmother had died the

previous year. Her mum and dad had wanted Amy's grandpa to come and live with them afterwards, but he'd refused.

'This is my home,' he'd insisted, his voice cracking. 'I've lived here for forty years. I don't want to move.'

'But what about the war, Grandpa?' Amy had asked him.

Grandpa clenched his bony fists. 'I'm not being forced out of my home by Mr Hitler or anyone else,' he'd said.

'Misty's not here,' said Jack, coming into Amy's room and interrupting her thoughts. 'I've looked everywhere, but the front door was still open.'

'She must have run off,' Amy said, and she didn't blame Misty at all. To a dog it must have seemed as though the sky were exploding.

'We've got to find her!' said Jack.

'Wait!' their mother cried as Amy followed Jack downstairs and out of the house. 'You can't go. What if there's more bombs? What if you get hurt?'

'I'm eighteen, Mum, and going off to war in the morning,' said Jack. 'I can take care of myself.'

Mrs Dolan bit at her bottom lip. She loved Misty, but her children were far more important to her.

'We'll be OK, Mum,' Amy said. 'If the air-raid

siren goes off, we'll duck into one of the public shelters.'

The thought of them reassured Mrs Dolan.

'OK, but be careful,' she called out as they ran down the path. 'And don't go too far!'

As Jack and Amy ran off along the smoke-filled street, people emerged from their homes, shocked and frightened, looking for company.

'Why today . . . ?'

'I was just having a cup of tea . . .'

'Lucky I bought those candles . . .'

By seven o'clock it was dark, the sun had set and the blackout had begun. Every window and door was covered with heavy blackout curtains, cardboard or paint. It had seemed like a nuisance before tonight, but not any more. No one wanted a glimmer of light escaping from their home to lead the enemy aircrafts' bombs straight to them. Even the street lights were either turned off or dimmed.

Jack and Amy hurried on down Lordship Lane stopping anyone they could.

'Excuse me, have you seen a dog?'

Most people didn't stop or even bother to answer them. They were too intent on getting home and checking on their loved ones, especially now it was getting dark.

'She's about this big.' Amy put her hand just above her knee.

'She's cream-coloured,' Jack said to a woman, who brushed past him saying she couldn't help when she realized he was talking about a dog. 'One ear goes up and the other one goes down . . .'

'And she's pregnant,' added Amy.

When they did manage to interest someone long enough for them to stop, rather than push on past, their description wasn't much help.

'So what breed is she?' a man wearing a trilby hat and a beige raincoat asked them.

'Well, she's mostly collie, but she's not black and white like a sheepdog.'

'She's creamy-coloured with floppy ears . . .'

Amy remembered Misty's sodden fur during their last holiday. 'She loves swimming!'

'That's a lot of help,' the man said.

Amy was stung. 'I'm sorry, I . . .' But the man had already moved on.

'It's OK,' Jack told her. 'He's just frightened. People act mean when they're scared.'

The blackout hampered their chances of finding Misty. Even traffic lights and vehicle headlights had special slotted covers to deflect the beams downwards so they wouldn't be so noticeable.

'Look out!' Jack said, grabbing Amy's arm as she was just about to step off the pavement.

Amy stepped back. She was so worried about

Misty that for a second she hadn't looked and not looking in the blackout could be fatal. Her teacher at school, Mr Dumphrey, was always warning them about this.

'Best thing you can do in a blackout is stay indoors,' he'd said.

But Amy and Jack couldn't do that, not tonight, not when Misty had gone missing. Amy couldn't bear to think of her out there in the dark, lost and afraid.

'If only Misty was a cat,' she said as she half ran to keep up with Jack's longer stride.

'What? Why?' said Jack, glancing over at his sister, but not breaking step.

'She'd be used to going out at night then . . . And everyone knows cats have good eyesight.'

A cat would be unlikely to get run over by a car, but Amy wasn't so sure about Misty.

They were almost at Wood Green Underground Station.

'She must be terrified,' Jack said, biting at his thumbnail as they passed the station clock.

Amy had a horrible, stomach-churning feeling of guilt that somehow it was her fault. She'd promised Jack she'd look after Misty while he was gone, and he hadn't even left yet and already his dog was lost.

'Misty . . . Misty . . . !' she called out into the blackness.

At least there weren't regulations against making a sound in the blackout, or not yet anyway.

A woman came out of the station and almost bumped into Amy.

'Oops, sorry, dearie – didn't see you there,' she said.

That was the problem. The blackout meant it was hard enough to see a person when they were almost on top of you. How on earth were they going to find a lost dog?

A man, wearing an Air Raid Precautions warden's uniform and tin hat, held up his hooded torch and they stopped as he peered at them.

'Who's Misty?' the ARP warden asked them.

'Our dog,' Jack told the man. 'She got frightened by the bombs and ran away.'

'She's pregnant,' added Amy. 'We've been looking everywhere for her. Have you seen her?'

'Dog you say? Who'd let a dog go out by itself on a night like this?'

Amy thought the ARP warden made it sound like Misty had gone waltzing off for a night on the town with some of her dog friends. Didn't he see how serious it was?

'I know someone who might be able to help you,' the warden said quickly when he saw the desperate looks on their faces. 'He'll see you right if anyone can, if he's not out looking for lost animals himself tonight. Works for NARPAC . . .'

'What's NARPAC?' Amy asked him.

'The animal side of my lot – stands for National Air Raid Precautions Animals Committee.'

'Oh.' Amy was glad they had wardens out there looking after animals too.

'It's made up of regulars from all the different animal welfare organizations, as well as a whole host of volunteers,' he told them.

'Like the RSPCA?' Amy asked. They'd collected money for the Royal Society for the Prevention of Cruelty to Animals at school.

'Yes,' the warden said, ticking the organizations off on his fingers. 'And the PDSA.'

'People's Dispensary for Sick Animals?'

'Lots of different groups came together to make NARPAC.'

And with that he set off into the darkness.

As night fell and the enforced blackout began, Misty padded along the terribly dark streets with her head down. Her strong sense of smell told her whenever anyone was close by, but a sudden jarring contraction pain deep in her tummy distracted her. She didn't have enough warning when the car with the blacked-out headlights hurtled towards her.

It bore down on her like some monstrous roaring beast and for a moment she just stood there. At the last second she jumped out of the way and ran for the pavement. But she wasn't quite quick enough and the car caught her rear end, spinning her around. She yelped in agony as she stumbled away from the beast that had now squealed to a stop.

'Hello, are you all right? Can't see a thing in this blasted blackout,' a voice called into the darkness.

Misty crouched low and a few seconds later the road creature rumbled and roared away. But there were others making the same sounds. She'd heard the noise before of course, but hadn't paid attention to it. That was before she knew these roaring creatures could also bring pain.

Her hind right leg and her back and belly hurt. She was tired, so very tired, and wanted to go home. But she'd come too far and didn't know the way back. The sharp pain in her tummy came again making her whimper.

Just at that moment she smelt a new smell. A smell that made her hackles rise and her body tremble. Then a growl came from the darkness in front of her. A dog, taller than Misty, thin but wiry with muscle and strong, appeared on the path in front of her, baring its teeth and slavering. It looked wild and unkempt and, unlike Misty, wore no collar. It let out another low, menacing growl.

Thinking of her puppies, Misty turned and ran, her tail between her legs in terror. In spite of the pain she was in, adrenalin from fear drove her onwards. But she could hear the other dog chasing her. She'd never been in a fight, never been so much as confronted by another dog before.

It had almost caught her, and was so close Misty could smell its foul breath, when the ear-splitting crash of a bomb stopped them both and everyone around them.

The other dog turned and ran across the road in blind panic. Misty crawled into the nearest hiding place, a narrow tunnel at the back of Wood Green Underground Station. She cowered inside the tunnel, her tongue lolling out as she panted. If the slavering dog came back now, she would have no chance of escape.

But it didn't come back and, as the minutes on the station clock on the wall ticked by and the all-clear siren sounded, Misty's panting finally slowed. For the time being she was safe. Exhausted, she slept a little, only to be woken by another piercing pain deep inside her that made her yelp and then whine in misery as it increased. Misty knew it was time for her puppies to be born.

She slowly crawled deeper and deeper into the access tunnel and then froze in fear. She wasn't alone. A pair of luminous gold eyes stared straight at her.

Chapter 3

The ARP warden led Jack and Amy briskly down the road, turned a corner and then another before stopping in front of a house at the end of a terrace. The house was in total darkness, as were all the others in the street, because of the blackout.

'I think this is it, number thirty-nine,' he said, barely able to see the numbers in the darkness.

When the knock came, Mrs Ward put down her chopping knife, wiped her hands on her apron and headed for the front door. She didn't turn on any lights because of the blackout and so the floral papered hallway was in darkness. She opened the door to find Jack, Amy and Len, the local ARP warden, standing there. Len tipped his tin hat to her.

'Hello, Len,' she said, recognizing him. 'What can I do for you?'

'We've lost our dog,' Amy said immediately.

'Oh, you poor dears, you must be so worried. Come on in. My husband should be back soon.

He's taken Michael and Ellie with him to Shoreham Road to see if they can help – the whole street has been badly hit.' A look of worry passed across Mrs Ward's face, but she quickly shook her head, smiled and held the door open for them.

Jack and Amy didn't know who Michael or Ellie were, but the lady seemed kind and so they went into the house. The first thing Amy noticed was that it smelt like a pet shop. There was even a bale of hay by the front door.

'Coming in for a cup of tea, Len?' Mrs Ward asked the ARP warden. But he shook his head.

'Got to be getting back, but I'll take you up on that offer next time I'm in the area.'

'Any time, Len,' said Mrs Ward, and she closed the door and led Jack and Amy inside.

Amy had never seen so many pets all together in one room before. There was a miniature poodle, a black and brown King Charles spaniel and a German shepherd lying on a rug by the hearth. She counted at least ten cats, all of different breeds, sitting on shelves and chairs and the window sill. There were bird cages with canaries and budgies in them and even two guinea pigs!

'You've got tons of pets,' Amy said with admiration.

'There're chickens and goats and rabbits outside in the garden,' Mrs Ward told her.

'Wow! You're so lucky,' said Amy. She sank down

on to the sofa that Mrs Ward indicated and Jack sat down next to her. The sofa even had cushions with dogs and cats embroidered on them.

'Oh, they aren't all our pets, dear.' Mrs Ward smiled. 'They're from all over. It's on account of my husband's work with NARPAC. We've got used to people asking if we can take in a pet they can't look after any more. The animal-rescue centres are so overcrowded, you see, and I can't bear to turn them away. But we really don't have any more space – and they all have to be fed!'

An elderly yellow Labrador came over to them, thick tail wagging. Amy stroked her.

'She's our official meeter and greeter, aren't you, Heggerty?' Mrs Ward said, smiling fondly at the dog.

Heggerty slowly climbed up on to the sofa and lay down between Jack and Amy.

'Don't mind her,' said Mrs Ward as the dog made herself comfortable.

Meanwhile Mr Ward drove the NARPAC ambulance down the blacked-out streets towards the Shoreham Road bomb site.

Beside him sat seventeen-year-old volunteer Ellie Jones. She had her Airedale terrier Grace with her.

It was the first 'real' mission red-headed Ellie had done, although they'd had lots of dummy runs. As soon as the all-clear sounded, she'd raced out of the house. The Wards lived in the next street and Mr Ward already had the NARPAC ambulance engine running when she and Grace arrived. Mr Ward raised an eyebrow when he saw Ellie's dog was with her.

'She might be able to help,' said Ellie hopefully. 'Airedales were used as rescue dogs in the last war, and I've been training her up.'

Grace hopped into the ambulance after Ellie and settled at her feet.

'Hello,' Michael said from the back of the ambulance. He had Sky, the family's collie, with him.

Mr Ward sighed and drove off. He had far more passengers with him than he'd intended. Ellie was expected, but not her dog, and he'd had no intention of taking his thirteen-year-old son with him; Michael had been sitting in the back of the ambulance when he came out. Nor had he intended taking their black-and-white collie, Sky, but she'd raced out of the house and jumped into the animal ambulance as soon as Michael had opened the door.

'It's beautiful in an awful sort of way,' Ellie said as she looked out of the window up at the sky. It had an orange glow from all the fires that were burning.

Mr Ward steered the ambulance towards

Shoreham Road. The street had taken a direct hit and many houses had been badly damaged.

Their job was to try and find any pets that had survived and were now trapped in the bombed-out houses. But, as he drove, Mr Ward was all too aware that even if an animal survived the explosion the sheer terror of the experience might well prove fatal, especially for the smaller animals like guinea pigs and birds.

People had been told to put up notices on their front gates or doors saying how many people or pets were inside. But the notices were often blasted away by the bombs.

The local ARP warden came hurrying over as soon as Mr Ward pulled up.

'The owner of seventy-three's been taken to North Middlesex Hospital,' she said. 'But he said his poodle was upstairs under the bed.'

Number 73 had taken a direct hit and now the house looked more like a doll's house with the front taken off. It had set fire to the two houses either side of it.

Ellie, Michael and Mr Ward began to cough at the smoke and dust as soon as they climbed out of the ambulance. Ellie's green eyes stung and watered. Behind them Sky sneezed.

'Here, these should help,' said the ARP warden and she gave Ellie, Michael and Mr Ward damp rags to cover their faces.

All around them was chaos, with people yelling and a constant jangling as fire engines and ambulances arrived and left.

'Seventy-five and seventy-one have pets too,' the ARP warden shouted over the noise in the street. 'And seventy-five's got a cat called Night, but he wasn't sure if the cat was in the house or not when the bomb went off,' she added, checking her book. 'We've secured both houses so it should be OK to check them, but tread carefully.'

'I'll take seventy-five,' said Ellie, and she and Grace headed off.

'Sky and I will check in seventy-one,' Michael said.

Mr Ward didn't want him to, but he didn't want Michael coming into number 73 either. The house looked like it was only managing to stay up on a wing and a prayer. At least the ARP warden had given numbers 71 and 75 the OK.

'Mind your backs!' a fireman called out to them as he unravelled a hose.

Michael and Sky headed towards 71.

'I'll keep an eye on them,' said the ARP warden, and she set off after the boy and dog.

'Be careful,' Mr Ward called out.

All Michael had with him was a dimly lit torch and inside the house it was very dark. If a frightened animal were hiding and stayed hidden, there was little hope of it being found until it was light.

The darkness wasn't a problem for Sky however. Tail wagging, she set off, going from room to room.

'What is it, Sky? What is it?' Michael encouraged her as she stopped in what had once been the kitchen, but was now almost unrecognizable as such. Sky scratched at the rubble, whined and then barked. Michael and the ARP warden helped Sky while taking care not to move too much debris too quickly.

Sky scrabbled at the rubble and whined some more and, just as Michael thought he heard a faint sound, Sky's head went into the space they'd made and came out holding a tiny mewling kitten in her mouth.

'Good girl, Sky, good girl,' Michael said.

'Well, I'll be . . .' said the warden.

Michael took the kitten from Sky and gently checked it over. Apart from being covered in dust and its heart beating much too fast, the kitten seemed unharmed.

In number 75 Ellie and Grace worked carefully and methodically, going from room to room. The ARP warden had told them the owner had a black cat called Night.

'But he wasn't sure if the cat was in the house or not when the bomb went off,' she'd added.

'Night, are you in here? Where are you, puss?'

Ellie had a little chicken in her pocket to tempt

the cat out, although realistically she knew from her training that terrified animals didn't usually have much of an appetite.

Grace mostly stayed close, but occasionally she wandered off to sniff at something.

'Found something, Grace?' Ellie asked.

She was amazed at how calm the dog was. Ellie herself was frightened that one of the walls might collapse at any moment, or the ceiling might fall down on top of them, or that there'd be another bomb.

'You can't think about that now,' she told herself firmly. She was there to do a job and she was going to do it. 'Night, Night?' she called.

Grace stopped and barked at the foot of the stairs and Ellie peered up into the darkness, trying to see or hear what had alerted the dog. Her dipped torch didn't give out much light, but she could see that part of the banisters had come away and some of the stairs looked very damaged indeed.

'You think there's something up there?' said Ellie doubtfully.

Grace barked again and Ellie sighed. It looked dangerous, but she'd better check.

'Be careful,' she told Grace as the dog padded up the stairs behind her.

Grace stopped by the wardrobe in the main bedroom, looked up and barked again, then sat down, looked over at Ellie and whined.

Ellie shone her torch, but she still couldn't see Night, although she agreed with Grace that it was a good sort of hiding place for a cat. She had just climbed on the bed to have a better look behind some boxes when the light from her torch caught the reflection of a pair of green eyes, wide and alert in the darkness.

'Hello, Night,' Ellie said softly. 'Hello, boy.' She held out her hand to him, but Night was not in the mood to be soothed or stroked. He shrank away from Ellie's outstretched arm.

She held out a piece of chicken, hoping to tempt him, but with a yowl Night raked his paw at her, jumped down on to the bed and raced out of the room past Grace, who watched him go and then looked over at Ellie, her head cocked to one side.

'No, that wasn't supposed to happen!' said Ellie.

They went carefully down the stairs, but couldn't see the cat. The ARP warden was outside.

'Did you see the cat?' Ellie asked her.

'Yes – just ran past me – no chance of stopping it.'

Ellie smiled. 'Well, at least he wasn't injured – judging by how fast he was going!'

'I'll let the owner know,' the warden said. 'But I wouldn't be at all surprised if Night was waiting on the doorstep for his breakfast in the morning.'

Ellie hoped so, but she decided to come back to check in the morning, just in case the cat had been too frightened to come home.

They went to see how the others were getting on, Grace stepping carefully over the broken glass that was everywhere.

'Sky found a kitten!' Michael grinned as his father arrived at number 71 to help him. Mr Ward hadn't found anything in number 73.

'What a pretty pickle, what a pretty pickle,' said a voice out of nowhere.

They all looked round at number 71's living room, and for the first time noticed the dust-covered stand in the corner.

'Mummy's little *po-ppet.*'

Mr Ward carefully lifted the cover. The parrot was in a cage and squawked and hopped about, and then started to make growling sounds. He dropped the cover back down. The parrot would feel safer with it in place for the moment. Fortunately the bird didn't seem to be too injured, judging by its talkativeness. But it was obviously traumatized by the night's bombings.

'Let's be getting you home,' Mr Ward said as he carried the birdcage out to the NARPAC ambulance. Inside the cage the parrot made clicking sounds in its throat.

'Need any help?' Ellie asked from the blown-out doorway. Grace and Sky sniffed and wagged their tails at each other.

'No, I think we're just about done here,' said Mr Ward.

The ARP warden stroked Grace and patted Sky's head. 'What good dogs you are,' she told them.

Sky was so pleased with herself her tail was almost wagging in circles. She jumped into the back of the ambulance and Michael climbed in behind her carrying the kitten.

'Guess there'll be no stopping you and Sky from coming with me on rescue missions from now on,' said Mr Ward.

'Nope,' Michael agreed. The sight, smell and sounds of the bombed-out street had been terrible. But rescuing the kitten was something he'd never forget. He wanted to do it again.

'Some of the animals might be horribly injured,' Ellie warned him as she climbed in. But the next time she was needed she knew she'd be there too, even though at times it had felt like her lungs were bursting from all the smoke.

'And some won't even be alive,' she said sadly.

Grace put her head on Ellie's knee and looked up at her.

'I know,' said Michael. But he felt the same way as Ellie: nothing would stop him from helping an animal in need.

Ellie stroked Grace as they headed off. Her last-minute decision to bring her along had been a good one. Without her Night would have been trapped in the house.

Michael cradled the kitten all the way home and it was asleep by the time they turned the corner of their street.

Chapter 4

Inside the Wards' house Heggerty heard the sound of a vehicle drawing up outside, and almost before the engine had stopped she was off the sofa and out of the room, her tail wagging like a pendulum. She was waiting by the front door for them as Michael, his father, Ellie, Grace and Sky came in, dusty, dirty and smelling of smoke, to a cacophony of greetings from the other animals.

Ellie's red hair now looked grey from all the dust, her face had streaks of dirt down it and her hands were filthy.

'Hello, old girl,' Mr Ward said as he patted Heggerty with his free hand.

Although he'd much prefer it if Michael stayed safe at home, he intended to take Sky with him on rescue missions from now on. She did seem to be suited to the work and not fazed by going into a bombed building. But he would never take Heggerty.

Heggerty was almost fifteen and greying round her muzzle. Although she never turned down a walk or a play, she was not as absolutely desperate to go out as she had once been, especially first thing in the morning.

Sky raced past Heggerty and ran in a circle round Mrs Ward's feet before stopping in front of the visitors sitting on the sofa.

'Hello,' Michael said when he saw Amy and Jack. He wondered why Jack was wearing what looked like his dad's suit of all things, but he didn't want to be rude so he just smiled.

Jack nodded to him and pulled at the tie that was half strangling him, as if he could read Michael's thoughts. Jack's face flushed red when he saw Ellie. She had the prettiest green eyes he'd ever seen. She caught him looking at her.

'I must look a state,' she said, laughing.

'Not at all!' Jack exclaimed and then flushed as red as a beetroot.

Ellie went to wash her hands and face and Grace followed her. Sky took the opportunity to jump up into Amy's lap and lick her chin. Amy laughed and stroked her.

'Get down, Sky,' Mr Ward told her as he brought in the parrot, but Sky didn't listen to him.

Heggerty carefully climbed back on to the sofa in between Jack and Amy and put her head on Jack's leg.

'This is Jack and Amy. They're here about their missing dog,' Mrs Ward said.

'Right,' said Mr Ward. 'I'll be with you in just a minute.' He went to get a NARPAC form to write down their details.

From inside his coat Michael lifted out the kitten he'd found, and Mrs Ward took it from him and wrapped it in a towel as Sky jumped off the sofa, bounded over and licked at the small mewling creature.

'Without Sky I wouldn't even have known it was there, Mum,' Michael said as he gave Sky a stroke. 'Do you think she knows she's just saved that kitten's life, or do you think Sky thinks she's playing a giant game of hide-and-seek?'

'Whatever Sky thinks, it worked,' said Mr Ward, coming back in with the form.

He'd be sure to tell the other NARPAC volunteers what a difference taking along Sky and Grace had made. It should also strengthen the case for a national War Dog Training School, like there'd been in the Great War, to be started up again.

Ellie's dad had been badly injured in the Great War in the trenches of Picardy. He wouldn't tell his daughter much about the war because the memories were too distressing. But he had told her about the amazing things that highly trained dogs could do to help with the war effort. One of them had brought the first-aid equipment that had saved Ellie's dad's life. Ellie was determined to see a national War Dog Training School set up, and examples of what even pet dogs like Grace and Sky had done tonight would only strengthen the case.

'There, there, you're all right, you're safe now,' Mrs Ward told the trembling kitten.

'And look what I got for my trouble,' Mr Ward added as he pulled the cover off the parrot's cage.

'Who's a pretty boy then, who's a pretty boy,' the parrot chirped.

It wasn't covered in dust like the kitten had been, thanks to the cover over its cage, but it had no water and no food.

Mr Ward opened the cage door to refill its water bowl and the parrot nipped at his finger.

'Ouch!' he said as he put his bleeding forefinger in his mouth. 'That's gratitude for you.'

'Mummy's little *po-ppet*,' the parrot chirped, making Michael, Amy and Jack laugh.

'That parrot's got attitude,' said Michael, minding his fingers as he pushed a slice of apple through the bars of the cage. 'Here you go – thirst-quenching and tasty at the same time.'

Mr Ward turned back to Jack and Amy, and wrote Misty's name on the top of the NARPAC form.

'Now when did she go missing?' he asked.

'When the air-raid siren went off,' said Amy. 'Misty must have been terrified.'

'Poor thing,' agreed Michael. 'I was terrified and I knew what was happening.'

Amy nodded. 'We're really worried because she's pregnant and Jack's going away to war tomorrow.'

'The army?' Mrs Ward said, looking over at the boy in the suit that was too big for him. He seemed much too young to be joining up, hardly older than her Michael.

Jack's face flushed red as Ellie and Grace came back in. He nodded.

Mrs Ward gave the kitten in the towel to Amy to look after and went to the kitchen to prepare some food for them all. She was angry as she chopped up a carrot and an apple for the parrot, cut a little fish for the kitten and slapped dripping on the bread for sandwiches. Boys like Jack being sent off to war – it just wasn't right!

'And has Misty ever run off before?' Mr Ward asked Jack and Amy.

'Oh no.'

'Never,' confirmed Amy as the kitten peeped out from the towel at her.

'She's not that sort of dog,' added Jack.

Mrs Ward came back in with the carrot, apple, fish and sandwiches.

Jack and Amy looked at the sandwiches hungrily, but didn't take one until Mrs Ward said, 'Go on, help yourselves. I made them for you too.'

Michael saw the parrot eating the carrot and apple and smiled to himself. There didn't seem to be too much wrong with the bird.

'Misty's puppies will be all right, won't they?' asked Amy.

Ellie, who'd already felt pity for the frightened runaway, was now really concerned.

'She's wearing her collar and ID tag, isn't she?' Michael asked Jack and Amy.

Amy nodded. 'Yes, Mum registered her. So Misty's wearing the collar and ID tag with the number on it that she was given.'

'Good,' said Mr Ward. At least that was something. Before the war a national register had been set up and registered animals were issued with a NARPAC numbered disc attached to a collar as identification.

'If you had a photo with her in it, it might help to jog people's memories when we look for her,' said Michael. 'But I don't expect . . .'

'We do!' Amy interrupted him. Like most people the Dolans didn't have many photos, but they did have one of Misty.

'Good,' said Mr Ward. Sky dropped one of her balls on top of the form in his lap and he threw it across the room for her to chase after.

'I hope we find her before she has her pups,' Amy said.

'Misty being pregnant makes it even more critical that we find her as quickly as possible,' said Mr Ward.

'Poor Misty, all alone,' Amy said, wiping away a tear. 'Will she be all right?'

Ellie and Michael exchanged a look.

'There's no time to lose,' said Mr Ward. 'She could need urgent medical attention if those pups decide to come along. But don't worry, she can't have got far – lost dogs tend to move in a triangle, so often don't end up that far from home.'

Amy bit her bottom lip hard to stop more tears from coming.

'I'll head out and search the area now,' Mr Ward said, picking up a sandwich to take with him.

'I'll come with you,' said Ellie.

'Me too,' said Michael.

'You two head back home now and see if Misty's returned,' Mr Ward told Amy and Jack. 'Let us know straight away if she has so we can call off the search.'

'We will,' Amy said as they hurried out of the door.

'Try rattling her box of biscuits as you call her name,' Michael called after them.

Jack and Amy ran all the way home, hoping against hope that Misty would be there, tail wagging, waiting for them.

'Is Misty back?' Jack asked as soon as he and Amy burst through the front door.

Mrs Dolan shook her head. 'Sorry, son, we've been out and asked all the neighbours, but there's been no sight or sound of her.'

Jack reached for Misty's biscuit tin, determined to go out and look for her again.

'I'm coming with you,' Amy said.

'No!' said Mrs Dolan. 'It's too dangerous. I . . .'

Her words were interrupted by the wail of an air-raid siren.

'Not again!' she cried as they ran for the Anderson shelter. They hadn't even cleared up properly from the last raid yet.

Amy sat, wide awake, inside the cold, damp shelter, holding Misty's tin of biscuits and listening to the foreboding hum of the planes, the shriek of the bombs as they fell, then the explosive crash as they landed.

This raid was even longer than the first and seemed to go on and on well into the night through to the early hours of the morning. Finally the all-clear siren sounded. Amy felt sick with tiredness and desperation as they went back to the house.

Misty must be almost crazed with terror out on the streets by now. How would she survive?

Chapter 5

Sheba the one-eared grey and black tabby cat had been born in the barn of a farm down in Kent almost eight years ago. Her first memories were of chasing mice and rats with her brothers and sisters, and the smell of hay and chickens and softly lowing cattle. But then, still a kitten, she'd been chosen and taken away from her mother and brothers and sisters to live an urban cat life in London with Mrs Collins.

From then on she'd had to live mainly indoors. When she did catch a mouse or a rat, and once or twice even a bird, the reaction from Mrs Collins had been one of horror rather than the pleasure Sheba had expected.

Mrs Collins had put a bell on the hated collar Sheba was forced to wear round her neck.

When the war came, Mrs Collins went away. Sheba waited all day and night on the window sill, but no one let her in, or gave her any food or water. Sheba hadn't minded this one little bit.

She'd managed perfectly well once she was alone and hunting for herself. Wood Green Station had become her new home and provided her with more than enough rats to eat. She'd lived in the Underground for longer than most of those that came to join her. It was so long ago now that she could barely remember the feeling of human hands stroking her.

Sheba wasn't in the least frightened when she came face to face with Misty in the dark ventilation tunnel. Very little frightened Sheba – and certainly not an injured, pregnant dog.

But, as Misty slowly crawled towards the cat's bright eyes ahead of her, little whimpers and cries of pain came from the dog. Sheba made a soft soothing sound that her mother had once made, a sound that told Misty she had nothing to fear.

But the pain that throbbed inside Misty was now almost too much for her to bear.

Sheba had seen other cats giving birth before and a dog wasn't so different. She stayed close to Misty during the hour or so it took for first one and then a second pup to be born. Her presence calmed the new mother. Both pups were boys and, although Misty was cream–coated, her puppies were white with tan patches.

Afterwards, in the relative safety of the narrow ventilation access tunnel, Misty licked her two tiny newborn pups clean. Like all puppies, they'd been born blind and deaf and toothless. They made mewling sounds as they pressed themselves close to their mother to keep warm.

Misty made a sound she'd never made before as she nuzzled her pups. It was a low, steady, happy growl of pure love. Almost a hum.

Hers was the first smell the pups recognized. It was the smell of love and warmth and food and safety. Outside the sirens wailed and the bombs dropped, but inside the tunnel the young puppies were oblivious to it all, snuggled up against their mum's side.

Three hours later Jack, Amy and their parents walked to the Underground.

Wood Green station stood proudly at the busy junction of Lordship Lane and the High Street. It was only eight years old and there'd been a grand opening ceremony for it in 1932 that they'd all gone to. The front of the station was curved and it had two ventilation towers to the left and right.

Despite almost everyone getting no sleep the night before, the station was surprisingly busy when Jack and his family arrived. The elderly man selling newspapers was doing a roaring trade.

'Read all about it! Read all about it!' he shouted, holding out newspapers and taking money.

Chaos as London is struck by Hitler's bombs! was written on the newspaper board.

'We'll never let Hitler win,' people around Jack said, although everyone agreed they wouldn't want a repeat of the night before.

Jack wished he didn't have to leave before they'd found Misty, but he didn't have a choice.

They went into the curved ticket hall and down the escalator to the platforms below.

'I'll keep looking for her when you've gone,' Amy promised him. 'I won't give up until I find her.'

Jack gave a tired smile. 'I know you won't,' he said.

'Write when you can,' said Mrs Dolan as she hugged him to her.

'There might not be much time,' he warned her as she blew her nose on a tear-sodden handkerchief.

His father shook his hand. 'Be well, son and make sure you change your socks regularly. Trench foot was a terrible blight in the Great War.'

'I will, Dad.'

'Let me know as soon as you find her,' Jack made Amy promise him, once again, as he boarded the Tube. 'Tell me as soon as you hear anything at all.'

'I will.'

Jack gave her his treasured black-and-white photograph of Misty.

'This should help.'

Amy took it from him, knowing that he'd

intended to take the photograph with him to basic training camp and on to wherever he was sent next.

'I don't need it to remember Misty,' he said. 'I could never forget her. And Mr Ward said it might be helpful in the search for her.'

The Tube train pulled out and Amy waved until it had gone, knowing that Jack probably couldn't see her, but not wanting to let a single tear slip down her face until the train had left the station.

If only she'd known just how close Misty was to them at that moment: she was just a few feet away, hidden from view in the narrow tunnel with her two newborn pups.

Misty heard the voices of people wafting through the walls of the station. Some voices even sounded familiar to her, but she was too preoccupied with her puppies to go and investigate. They were the most important thing to her now and she would do anything for them.

The pain in her back and leg from being hit by the car had grown much worse, but the puppies' needs came first. Misty fed her pups, cleaned them and then slept.

When she awoke later, she was ravenously hungry. Hungrier than she'd ever been in her life. She needed to eat, but she couldn't leave the puppies for any length of time as they were totally dependent on her for everything. She sniffed the station air and her sensitive nose caught the smell of food. It was a strange mixture, some of which she'd tasted: bread and eggs, bacon fat, lard; and some of which she'd never smelt before, but knew was definitely food. And it was close. Her stomach rumbled. She knew she desperately needed to eat to regain her strength if she were to be able to feed her pups.

Misty crawled out of the ventilation tunnel leaving the two pups sleeping and let her nose lead her to a small yard at the back of the station where the pig bins were kept. She'd found the source of the smell.

To the station staff's noses the pig bins smelt awful, so they put them round the back of the station with an arrow directing people to their new spot – downwind. Flies loved the smell coming from the pig bins and swarms of bluebottles buzzed round them, but that didn't put Misty off. To her sensitive nose the smell of the food was droolingly overpowering.

The bins had lids on them and it was impossible for Misty to reach them without standing up on her hind legs. But when she tried she yelped in pain as her injured leg gave way. Suddenly she crouched in fear as a hand reached out from above her and removed the lids for her. Before she had time to run away the bin itself was on the ground, its contents spilling out, and the hand was gone and Misty was eating and eating and eating – a bit of pie, some cake, bread, bacon, chicken, half a sausage. She gulped down the food as fast as she could, not even chewing it, until her belly was full to bursting.

Then she went back to her pups and the bluebottles went back to buzzing round the bins.

Once she'd gone, nineteen-year-old Daniel came back out of the shadows. His meals came from the pig bins too. But unlike Misty Daniel always made sure to put the lids back on and tried to get to the food as soon as possible after it was thrown away so it wasn't too spoilt.

'Hello, puss,' he said to the one-eared cat he found watching him from a ledge. He stretched out a hand, but Sheba ran away after Misty before he could stroke her.

Daniel had lived in the station long enough to know how to be mostly invisible to the staff, although he couldn't have said exactly how long he'd been there. The concept of time seemed to have become lost to him ever since he'd been hiding in the station tunnels, which had become his home. Now each day drifted foggily into the next one with his only imperative being to find food when he needed to, and to remain hidden.

Now Misty had had her fill, Daniel checked each of the bins and helped himself to a half-eaten loaf of rock-hard stale bread from the staff canteen and some cake that was a bit soggy because it had been next to some cabbage leaves, but was otherwise fine.

Daniel took his makeshift meal back to the small, dusty, disused room he'd claimed as his own. There had been plans to use this part of the station as offices and the room still had a table and an office chair in it, along with a telephone that was disconnected. Daniel had added sacking to the ground to sleep on and made it his home.

The electric light didn't work, but that was fine by Daniel. He liked the darkness – it made him feel safer. In the dark he couldn't be seen as he had been in France, seen and shot at by the German soldiers.

Once he'd been so eager to play his part in the war effort and help lead England to victory. Now that time seemed like another lifetime ago and all he wanted to do was forget. Only he couldn't. The terrible memories were always there, haunting him.

Daniel pulled off chunks of the bread and ate them. The rats would finish whatever he didn't eat. He only ever took meat if he was sure it hadn't been in the pig bin for very long. A stomach upset after eating leftover chicken had taught him that it just wasn't worth it.

Sometimes people walked past the room, but

not often; there was no reason for anyone to come inside. Nevertheless he always ducked into the shadows and kept very still when he heard the sound of footsteps.

His hair had grown long during the months he'd been down there, and his face was grubby with the dirt that had built up from not washing properly. Most people would not have recognized him as the eager young soldier he'd once been, proudly going off to war.

The puppies were awake and crying pitifully and loudly for her when Misty came back from her first trip to the pig bins. She'd only been gone for a short while, but they were lonely and cold, unable to keep themselves warm. When she got back, Misty smelt different to her blind and deaf pups. She smelt of cake and eggshell and stale bread and pastry and gravy and jam. The puppies, however, were only interested in Misty's milk, especially the firstborn pup who was always hungry.

Misty fed both pups and then meticulously cleaned them as she did after each meal and whenever they woke up. Stomachs full and warmed by their mum, the puppies soon drifted back to sleep. Misty slept too, but fitfully, and she whimpered with the pain in her leg and a new pain that was developing deep inside her.

She could still smell Daniel and knew he was

somewhere very near, but she sensed that he meant her and her pups no harm.

Sheba lay close by and kept a careful watch over them all.

Chapter 6

Amy took Misty's photograph and tin of dog biscuits with her as she headed back to the Wards' house through the bomb-damaged streets. Firemen had put out the fires from the night before and were now rolling up their hoses, but they couldn't wash everything away. Broken window glass and wood, bricks, paper, dust and dirt remained.

People called to each other as they swept up the broken glass and boarded up their windows. The bomb damage had everyone talking and sharing their experiences. Neighbours helped each other with their repairs. Cups of tea and hammers and nails were shared.

The smoke that lingered in the air from the previous night's fires made Amy cough and she worried that there might be an air-raid warning siren going off at any time, but she'd promised Jack she'd find Misty and she intended to do just that.

She'd never forget how excited she and Jack had been the day their father had brought Misty home, a bundle of fur and big brown eyes, in a wicker basket. Misty had been just ten weeks old, Amy had been six and Jack had been twelve that very day. Misty had been a birthday present.

'What do you think of her then?' their father had said as Jack lifted Misty out of the basket and held her to him.

Amy was in total awe of the puppy. 'She's so beautiful,' she'd said.

Once she'd sat down, Jack had handed her Misty to hold. She'd marvelled at how soft Misty's fur was and laughed when the puppy licked her face.

Both she and Jack had thought Misty was perfect from the moment they'd met her. The first time they'd taken her to the seaside she'd loved digging in the sand. But when she saw Jack and Amy going into the sea she'd barked and barked. It was as if she were warning them to be careful. When they didn't come back, she'd splashed into the waves, for the very first time, to join them and soon they were all swimming together. It was the best holiday ever and they all went swimming every day.

Amy smiled at the memory. Every good memory she had, in fact, had Misty prominently in it somewhere.

Amy pulled the photograph from her pocket and showed it to anyone who would stop for long enough to look.

'Excuse me, have you seen this dog . . . ? She's

cream-coloured . . . she went missing last night . . . she's quite shy.'

Amy had almost given up hope of anyone having seen Misty when a woman wearing a bottle-green scarf said she thought she might have done.

'Poor little thing. I was just coming out of the station when I saw her. I wanted to stop, but my friend urged me on and so I didn't – I wish I had. She must have been so frightened,' the woman said. 'She seemed shy, almost hesitant . . .'

A tear slipped down Amy's face and she brushed it away with her fingers because she didn't have a handkerchief with her.

'She was . . . is, I mean.'

'I hope you find her,' the woman said.

Amy nodded and sniffed. 'I hope so too, thank you.' At least someone had seen Misty and there was now a little more hope that she might find her.

She turned down the street that led to the Wards' house and knocked at their door. The dogs inside barked excitedly.

'Amy,' Mrs Ward said as she opened the door. Amy was instantly surrounded by interested dogs. 'Give her some space, Sky. Heggerty, leave her alone. Has your brother left? Is there any news on Misty?'

'Yes and no,' said Amy as she went inside.

Mr Ward was out, but Michael was there. He

came in from collecting chicken eggs in the back garden.

Amy told him and Mrs Ward that someone had seen Misty. 'Where?' Michael asked.

'Near the station. Yesterday your dad said something about lost dogs moving in a triangular pattern and I wasn't sure what he meant. How big would this triangle be?'

'It's usually a maximum of five miles,' Michael told her. 'But I don't think a pregnant dog like Misty would be able to go that far.'

'Here, this might help,' said Mrs Ward. She spread out a map of their area of London on the kitchen table.

'So if we start from your house in Swan Street...'

'That's here,' Amy said, pointing to it.

'And now we know she was seen near Wood Green Station . . . Then the third point of the triangle has to be . . .'

'Here,' Amy said, pointing at Alexandra Palace. She sighed. If Misty was lost there then she might be very hard to find, especially with London in such chaos with the bombings.

Alexandra Palace, or Ally Pally as everyone called it, had almost two hundred acres of parkland surrounding it.

'It's such a large area to search,' she said, sighing.

Michael nodded. The parkland was the perfect place for a dog to hide.

'Right, though of course Misty's route wouldn't be as straight or exact as the lines on a map,' he said.

At least now they knew roughly where to look and any plan was better than no plan.

'Did Misty have a favourite place she liked to go?' Michael asked Amy. If she did then it might be best to try there first.

'Definitely our local park,' said Amy. Lordship Recreation Ground was much nearer to their house than Alexandra Palace, and she and Jack often took Misty there. Jack had commented on how much she loved it when they'd passed the park on their way to the station earlier and suggested she keep looking there.

'Lordship Rec and a ball to chase were Misty's idea of heaven,' Amy added.

'Then that's where we should try first,' said Michael. 'I'll come and help you look.'

Sky wagged her tail hopefully.

'Come on then,' Michael said.

Heggerty wagged her tail too, but Michael looked doubtful. Heggerty wasn't able to manage long walks any more and he wasn't sure how long they'd be. But still he didn't like to say no to her.

'Not you, Heggerty,' said Mrs Ward. 'Come on, I've got some chicken you might like.'

Heggerty followed her into the kitchen as Amy, Michael and Sky left the house.

Amy yawned as they headed back up the streets she'd just come down.

'Oops – sorry,' she said.

'That's OK – no one got much sleep last night,' said Michael, smiling.

Sky wagged her tail. She didn't seem to be in the least bit tired.

Amy shook Misty's tin of biscuits, called out her name and showed people her photograph. But no one else had seen her and most people looked like they had other, more pressing things to worry about than a missing dog.

'The war has left so many pets homeless and unwanted,' said Michael as he saw Amy's look of despair. 'When it started, lots of people thought they wouldn't be able to look after their pets any more. Hundreds of thousands were put down at the start of the war and many more have been abandoned, left to wander the streets, and become strays. Dogs who'd once been loved now have to fend for themselves as best they can.'

'I feel so sorry for them,' Amy said. 'It's so unfair.'

Michael nodded his agreement.

'NARPAC can only do so much and, as the war continues, more and more pets need our help, especially with the bombings. But the truth is we can't help them all.'

'I don't want Misty to become like them,' said Amy.

And what would happen to Misty's puppies if she did? It was hard enough for an adult dog to survive. What chance would a vulnerable puppy have?

'At least she's registered; those that haven't been are at the very bottom of the list,' Michael said.

'I was supposed to look after Misty while Jack went to war. She was my responsibility. But she'd gone missing before he'd even left,' said Amy.

'That wasn't your fault,' Michael told her.

But Amy couldn't help thinking that it was. She swallowed hard.

'When the air-raid siren went off, I was so frightened I couldn't even think. I just ran for the Anderson shelter – I left Misty behind – so you see it was really my fault.'

'No,' Michael started to say again.

But Amy shook her head because whatever he said she couldn't forgive herself.

They went in through the metal gates of Lordship Rec and once Michael unclipped her lead Sky raced off to find a squirrel to chase. She came back with a broken, discarded shoe.

'That's not a ball!' Michael said, laughing.

'If only Sky could sniff something of Misty's and find her like those sniffer dogs do,' said Amy.

'Ellie's done scent training with Grace,' said Michael. 'She said dogs love it. Their noses are so super-sensitive I suppose it must seem like playing hide-and-seek to them.'

'I can't imagine trying to find someone just by sniffing,' Amy said with a grin.

'Me neither.'

'I like Ellie,' said Amy, remembering the pretty, friendly girl she'd met the night before. She smiled as she remembered that Jack had liked her too.

'Yeah, she's OK,' Michael agreed. 'She's off checking on a cat she rescued last night.'

Michael threw the shoe-ball for Sky as they went past the duck lake. The model traffic area had been closed at the start of the war but people were still cycling on the bike paths.

Amy saw several people she recognized from when she'd come to the park with Misty, but none of them had seen the dog.

'I'll keep a lookout,' one woman with a bulldog promised.

'Misty . . .' Amy called again and again. 'Misty . . .' But there was no sign of her.

Amy felt very low as they left the park. She'd been so hopeful that Misty might be there. What had happened to her? Had her pups been born yet and, if they had, were they all right? Were they . . .? No, she wouldn't even let herself think that they might not be all right.

From Lordship Rec they headed to the station and out towards Alexandra Palace. Sky trotted along happily on her lead and wagged her tail whenever Amy shook the biscuit tin.

'If only there was something more I could do to help all the other dogs too,' she said. 'If I could just help even one to find its way home, it might make not finding Misty . . .'

'Don't talk like that!' Michael said. 'Misty's only been lost for a day – you can't even begin to give up hope of finding her yet. Even in peacetime it can be weeks before a lost pet gets reunited with its owner and this is definitely not peacetime.

'At the start of the war my friends, Robert and Lucy, got evacuated down to Devon and their three pets stayed in London and do you know what happened?'

Amy shook her head.

'Months later his Jack Russell, Buster, turned up as a search-and-rescue demonstration dog and his cat, Tiger, and sheepdog, Rose, made it all the way from London to Devon, and I'm still not really sure how they did it.'

By now Amy's mouth was hanging open and she quickly closed it. 'That's amazing,' she said.

'If you really want to help, you should come along to one of the NARPAC meetings. Ellie usually does a dog-training class afterwards now that she's trying to get the national War Dog Training School started.'

'Really?' Amy said. 'I would like to help.'

'Well, we can do with all the help we can get,' said Michael with a grin.

They went up the hill that Alexandra Palace stood on. From the top they had a panoramic view of London.

'It's still beautiful,' said Amy as she looked out. So many people busily living their lives down below them.

Michael looked at the flames and smoke that still came from some of the buildings. Hundreds of homes and factories and schools had been destroyed the night before and countless people killed. But being up here gave London an ethereal air, like some kind of magic land that they weren't quite part of.

Sky raced after a honey-coated spaniel and they barked as they played together. The two dogs ran under the fence that enclosed the horse racecourse track and Michael and Amy went after them.

'One of my dad's jobs was to check on the horses that raced here,' Michael told Amy. 'He calls it the Frying Pan because of its shape.'

Amy looked up at the palace as they headed back down the hill. The transmitter tower stretched upwards. Her father had told her it was used to jam German bombing navigation systems. She hoped it had jammed them so badly they didn't work any more so the German planes never came back.

'Don't give up; sunrise and sunset are supposed to be the best times for finding a missing dog,' Michael told her. 'Or at least that's what my dad says. That's when it's most likely to return to its home.'

'Thanks for today. I think I'd better get back home now,' Amy said. 'But I'd like to come along to the NARPAC meeting.'

'Good,' said Michael as he and Sky headed off towards his house. He only wished they'd been able to help Amy find Misty.

Chapter 7

Inside the Underground station the narrow ventilation access tunnel where Misty had given birth to the pups was in many ways the perfect 'nest'. It was warm and dry, safe and relatively clean.

Misty's two pups didn't make much noise apart from soft grunts and squeaks, and even these they couldn't hear for themselves, nor see each other, as their eyes and ears weren't open yet. Their sense of smell, however, was fully developed.

Misty was a good mum and her puppies were healthy and well-fed with little round stomachs. They were everything to her and she made soft, lullaby-like growls deep in her throat to them.

Sheba brought Misty rats that Misty ate hungrily, although she'd never eaten one before coming to the station. She'd never, in fact, eaten any raw food before the rats she was given, but now she did.

Sheba also lay with the pups to help keep them

warm when Misty headed off to the pig bins. As the puppies cuddled up together, their tiny limbs twitched and waved and their little pink tongues went in and out as they made milk sucking movements.

But although Misty's puppies were strong and healthy, Misty herself wasn't. The pain from where the car had hit her had increased and, although she ate from the pig bins, she was losing weight rather than gaining it. At six she was old to have a first litter and giving birth to the puppies had taken its toll.

About two weeks after he was born, the larger of the two pups' eyes and ears opened and he saw their dark tunnel home and heard the whistle and rumble of the Underground trains for the first time. The next day his younger brother's eyes and ears opened and they saw each other.

The puppies were both tan-and-white coated, in comparison to Misty's cream coat. The firstborn was slightly larger and had a white tip to his right ear, but otherwise they were almost perfect copies of each other. They both had newborn blue eyes which would gradually change to brown.

Their legs weren't strong enough for either of them to be able to stand yet. But they were able to crawl by paddling their front legs to drag themselves along. The firstborn pup found his voice and barked. Previously he'd only managed to grunt and mew. He heard the bark and liked the sound; he tried it again and again.

The second puppy tried to bark too, but it came out as a yelp. He yelped again, but then the whistle of a Tube train passing made him throw his head back and turn that yelp into a howl. He was so surprised he paddle-crawled over to their mother who licked his furry head.

Although the puppies could now hear the bombs going off in the distance every night and often during the day as well, they thought nothing of them and certainly weren't frightened. It was all they'd ever known and so to them it was the way things should be.

A few days of paddle-crawling strengthened their muscles. Now they were able to crawl properly and soon the brothers were crawling over each other and their mother. Misty made her soft, happy growl and licked them.

In no time at all they were standing and taking their first wobbly steps. The older, larger puppy barked with excitement. The younger, smaller puppy yelped, apart from when a Tube train whistled: then he joined in with his high puppy howl.

The puppies were interested in everything about themselves, from their four paws, that they chewed and licked at, to their tails, which were particularly good entertainment when they ran in wobbly circles trying to catch them. They also tried to catch each other's tails, which usually resulted in a yelp as a tail got nipped by emerging teeth.

The station was their playground, and provided them with a range of tunnels and pipes to explore. Misty growled softly to warn them if ever they neared the forbidden 'people' territory. Sheba stayed close and kept watch over them too.

Daniel often heard the pups yapping excitedly as they played, and he liked to watch them from the shadows.

He named the pups Bark and Howl because of the different sounds they made. Sometimes he watched them for hours, hidden in the shadows or through a grill hole, but he never went close or tried to touch them. If he did, the cat with one ear hissed at him. She was always with them, taking care of the pups and watching over the little family. Misty had seen him watching them too and the soft growl she'd made deep in her throat gently told him to stay away.

Because he stayed hidden and rarely saw her at the pig bins any more, Daniel didn't know how sick Misty was. She was too ill now to eat much of anything. Her leg and back hadn't healed after the car had hit her and she was in constant pain. Sometimes she could barely stand and she was so thin that her ribs stuck out.

Sheba laid food close to her to try and tempt

her to eat. Sometimes Misty would take a little, but more often the puppies, now they were old enough, would gobble it up.

At night-time now, after she'd hunted and eaten, Sheba still chose to sleep close by Misty and her pups rather than with the other cats.

Besides Sheba there were about twenty other cats, and even more rats, living in the station. Bark and Howl tried to play with them, but usually they just ran away. Some of the cats were frightened of the pups and fled at the sight of them; others turned to face them, looking menacing, and from these cats the puppies ran. But, as the cats got used to the pups being there, more often than not a cat would simply give them a look before stalking off.

If needed, a warning sound from Sheba meant that none of the cats came too close or ever really threatened the puppies.

The pigeons made much better playmates than the cats or the rats. Bark and Howl raced down one rarely used platform that the pigeons roosted in, barking their high puppy barks. The birds scattered before them and Bark and Howl sneezed with puppy delight.

As they grew older, the puppies started to investigate the constantly changing pig-bin food. They were too small to get into the bins themselves, but Misty gathered what little strength she had left and, with their help and Sheba's, she managed to tip one over. Once the bin was on its side, Bark couldn't resist going right into it to see what he could find, sure that the tantalizing smell came from something buried somewhere inside.

Howl waited anxiously by the bin, listening as his brother ate. At last, Bark came out with his brown fur covered in cold porridge. Howl danced about in delight to see him and licked off the porridge with his little pink tongue.

A few days later Howl got covered in carrot curry and Bark returned the favour by licking him clean.

Often Bark or Howl would emerge with potato peelings on their heads. But they didn't get eaten with the same relish that the porridge and carrot curry had been.

One such day Sheba watched from a ledge on the wall as the puppies ate. She never chose to join in with the pig-bin feast herself – she much preferred a juicy rat.

Suddenly Sheba went deadly still at the sound of a low growl. The pups quickly looked round, but were too interested in eating to pay much attention to the noise. But Misty gave an instinctive whimper of fear and immediately moved to stand protectively in front of her pups and face what was coming.

Misty then gave a low warning growl, just as a large wiry dog came towards them out of the shadows, teeth bared. She instantly recognized the slavering beast as the feral dog she'd seen on the night of Bark and Howl's birth. Her neck hackles rose.

The feral dog was not in the least intimidated by Misty. She and her pups were no match for him. He was about to lunge at them when a voice shouted: 'Go on – be off with you!'

Misty didn't turn her head as she recognized the voice.

'Shoo!' Daniel shouted again, waving his arms this time. But the feral dog didn't leave. It just turned its huge head and growled at the man.

Daniel stared back into the beast's eyes. He knew the dog could attack him, but he also knew Misty and her pups would have no chance of survival without his help.

He pulled off the pig-bin lids and raised them like a shield as the dog turned towards him, its face twisted in a snarl. Daniel clashed the lids together, while slowly moving towards the dog, hoping to scare it away.

Misty took the chance to crawl into one of the narrow tunnels with Bark and Howl and lead them away to safety. They'd avoid eating from the pig bins again until she was sure it was safe for them to do so.

Daniel banged the lids together again and again at the dog. Each time it retreated a little further, until it finally turned and sloped off into the darkness.

When he looked round to check on the mother

and her pups, he was glad to see they'd gone. From the ledge above him he heard a miaow and saw the one-eared cat watching him.

'Hello, puss,' he said and stretched out his hand to her, although he knew she probably wouldn't allow him to stroke her.

But today Sheba pushed her head under Daniel's hand and purred her approval of what he'd done to protect Misty and her pups.

Hopefully the dog wouldn't come back to the pig bins again. But Daniel couldn't be sure about that. The beast was obviously hungry and the pig bins were full of food.

Safely back in their den, Bark and Howl were shaking with fear and making little whimpering cries. Misty licked them over and over to reassure them and herself. Finally they calmed down and fell asleep, but their dreams were marked with twitching and cries. Misty lay close to her pups and watched over them, but didn't sleep. She was now in constant pain and worried that the feral dog would return.

Sheba came to join her and washed herself close by.

Chapter 8

Ellie and Grace had come to pick Amy up for the NARPAC training class.

'Thank you for having me along. When Michael told me about the classes and the War Dog Training School, I thought it was such a good idea. It feels like I'll be helping Jack too, somehow,' Amy told Ellie.

'I know, it's a great cause and really important,' said Ellie, smiling. 'I'm hoping Lieutenant Colonel Richardson will think that too and set up the new national War Dog Training School soon so we can have trained dogs to help us win the war.'

'Who's Lieutenant Colonel Richardson?' Amy asked.

'The hero who set up the War Dog Training School in the last war,' Ellie told her.

Before Mrs Dolan would let them leave, she made sure Amy remembered where every overground and underground public shelter in the area was.

'And be careful,' she warned the girls.

'We will,' Ellie told her.

'It feels like we'll be helping Misty too, in a strange way. Poor Misty must be terrified, out there all alone,' Amy said when they were on their way.

No one had seen Misty since the night she'd gone missing.

'Most dogs would be,' agreed Ellie. 'That's why we need a proper War Dog School to train those that aren't.'

As they made their way to the Scout hut where Ellie ran the classes, she told Amy about how she used Grace to show people just what a properly trained dog could do. Before the war began, Grace and Ellie had often won first place in competition obedience classes. Ever since she'd been a pup, all Grace had really wanted to do was be with Ellie. Wherever Ellie went, Grace was happiest if she was close behind. But she was also obedient and if Ellie told her to stay she would – reluctantly.

Because of her knowledge of obedience training, Ellie ran the dog-training side of things for their local branch of NARPAC, which was how she knew the wardens, as well as giving people advice about their dogs.

Ellie believed that dog training should be a pleasure for both the dog and its owner. She didn't agree with those who thought stern discipline, a firm hand and a clip round the dog's head when it got something wrong were what was needed.

Brute force never got the best out of anyone. She wanted a dog that could think for itself and not be so frightened that it cowered away when anyone came near it.

Amy had often walked past the corrugated-iron-roofed Scout hut, with the fleur-de-lis emblem over the door, but she'd never been inside before.

As she, Ellie and Grace went through the swing doors, they were greeted by the sight of five dogs, of various breeds, and their owners. Michael, Mr Ward and Sky were already there. Sky and Grace greeted each other nose to nose, tails wagging.

The class began with a reminder of the basics: sit, down, stay, wait, come and don't touch. 'Don't touch' was very important for a dog that was going to help in rescue work to learn. There would be lots of opportunities in bombed-out houses to eat all sorts of things and no one wanted their dog getting poorly from eating mouldy leftovers!

Once they'd gone over the basics, it was time to play hide-and-seek and Amy had to find places to hide herself. The dogs, however, especially Grace, had played the game lots of times before and were always able to find her. They were supposed to bark and let their handler know when they found someone and Grace did. But, for most of the other dogs, finding Amy was so exciting that they forgot all about barking and jumped on her and licked her face instead.

Halfway through the class there was tea for the people and water for the dogs. In the break Michael left and came back with Heggerty, who Mr Ward used to demonstrate basic dog first aid on.

Heggerty took her role of first-aid dog demonstrator seriously and stood very still on the table while Mr Ward wrapped bandages round her. Once he'd shown everyone what they were supposed to do, they were invited to try it for themselves.

'Very fine work,' he told Amy as he watched her bandaging Heggerty's paw. 'You've got a knack for this.'

In no time at all it became Amy's job to do the first-aid demonstrations with Heggerty.

When it was Heggerty's turn to 'perform', she always slowly and carefully walked up the three steps to the stage, where she stood proudly, her tail wagging.

Once Amy had demonstrated how the bandaging was supposed to be done, anyone who wanted to give it a try themselves came out to the front. Heggerty was always extremely patient, even with those who were most fumble-fingered. Her favourite point of the evening, however, was teatime when she usually managed to persuade someone to share a bit of their sandwich or a biscuit with her.

Sometimes Mr and Mrs Dolan came along to watch Amy's demonstration.

'Anyone like to give it a try?' Amy asked, once she'd demonstrated how to bandage Heggerty's paw. Amy's dad put his hand up. He came out to the front and carefully wound the bandage as Heggerty helpfully held her paw up.

'We've very proud of you,' Mrs Dolan told Amy at the end of the class, squeezing her shoulder.

'I'm only showing people how to bandage an injured dog,' she said.

Her father shook his head. 'What you did was show them how to save a dog's life,' he told her.

Amy was very excited when they got home that afternoon and she received her first brief letter from Jack.

'*Had my army haircut,*' he'd written in his familiar scrawl.

What he didn't say was all that was now left of his hair was stubble.

'*Food's plentiful.*'

He didn't add that so far most evenings they'd had soggy corned-beef fritters for dinner.

'*Made some new friends.*'

Most of them were around the same age as him and all of them would be sent off to fight soon.

Amy wrote back to him telling him the news about helping Ellie and the War Dog Training School. She didn't mention Misty; it had been three weeks since she'd disappeared and Amy didn't know what to say, and, if she were honest, she didn't know what to do any more.

She then decided to write a letter to Lieutenant Colonel Richardson to ask him about starting the War Dog Training School again, and to tell him how good Ellie's classes were. At least that was something Amy could do to help.

Chapter 9

As each day passed, Bark and Howl grew stronger and more boisterous and confident in their underground home. They didn't know they'd never seen the sun or the moon or felt grass under their paws and they didn't care. The station was their world and they explored it as far as Misty and Sheba would allow them to.

Bark was always the more inquisitive and confident leader of the two, while Howl was happy to follow. It was Bark who first spotted the newspaper that had been blown into the station and wafted each time a train went past on another platform. Both puppies were frightened by the rustling sound it made.

Bark tentatively edged closer to the newspaper, his head cocked to one side. He stopped dead each time it moved and crept closer again once it was still. Howl watched his brother from a few feet away.

Once Bark had almost reached the newspaper, he barked at it. When it didn't respond, he put out his paw. Howl came running over and they both stared at the sheet and wagged their tails. There was nothing to be scared of here.

Newspaper discarded as neither friend nor foe, the puppies trotted on until they stopped dead at the sight of a glove on the ground.

They ran back to their mother and Misty staggered painfully to her feet and slowly went over and picked up the glove to show them there was nothing to fear from it. Her pain had grown so intense now and she was so weak from not eating properly that she couldn't stand for any length of time. She now spent days semi-conscious from the infection caused by the car injury to her back and leg. As she sank back down in pain, Bark grabbed the glove and it became a new toy for him and Howl.

When Daniel found anything he thought the puppies would particularly like, he saved it for them. A station worker left a ball of string behind one day and Daniel picked it up. He thought it'd make a fine ball for the pups and he hid behind the entrance to the disused platform and rolled it over to them.

Bark immediately raced up and pounced on it with Howl yapping excitedly behind him. But, as the puppies played with the string, it untangled like a ball of wool and spun out and along the platform.

Daniel put his hand over his mouth to stop

himself from laughing as even Sheba was unable to resist the string and was soon batting at it with her paws and chasing after it along with the puppies.

He longed to go out on to the platform and join them, but he was terrified of being seen by any of the station staff or passengers.

From where he stood, hidden, he couldn't see Misty lying further along the platform and didn't know how sick she had become.

Out on the platform Howl pushed his nose to Bark's and then backed away. Bark put a paw out to him and Howl play-bit at Bark's other forepaw, still on the ground. Soon the two pups were engrossed in play-fighting, biting at each other's legs, trying to gain dominance by pawing each other's backs and chewing each other's ears. Misty panted as she watched them and then closed her eyes and slept again.

Sometimes Bark and Howl were so tired they could only manage to play while lying down. Sleepily Bark would chew at Howl's ear in a slow-motion play fight. Then Howl would half-heartedly go for Bark's ear until finally they fell asleep lying half on top of each other – only to wake a little later, ready to begin playing again.

But, as the puppies thrived and grew strong, Misty grew ever weaker. Some days she could barely stand and then one morning, when the puppies awoke, Misty didn't get up. She lay where she was, on her side, chest rising and falling, occasionally giving a small whimper of pain.

Bark and Howl pawed at their mum and licked at her ears, but she still didn't sit up. Howl lay beside his mother, whining and licking her ear. Bark stood in front of her and barked, but Misty didn't even lift her head.

When Sheba came back from hunting through the broken grating, she found Misty lying on her side, her breathing laboured. Sheba went over to her and nuzzled her, but Misty barely reacted.

Then Sheba looked into Misty's glazed eyes and, as Misty stared back at her, her ragged breathing eased and she lapsed into a peaceful calm. Misty sighed and closed her eyes and didn't open them again.

Sheba made a sound deep in her throat and the puppies ran to her, confused as to why their mother was no longer moving. She led them away from Misty back towards the grating. Bark and Howl looked back at their mum and whimpered. They ran back to her and nuzzled her and licked her ears and face, trying to wake her. Sheba made the sound again and this time they followed her through the grating.

She fed the hungry puppies a freshly killed rat and then took them to the area of the station the cats had claimed as their own. They weren't too pleased to have the two puppies join them. One of them hissed and another cat raked out a paw as the puppies went past, but a hiss from Sheba stopped that behaviour.

Then they curled up together and went to sleep with Sheba lying beside them, keeping watch, as they whimpered for their mum in their sleep.

Daniel was sad when he came across Misty's body in the tunnel. She'd been a good mum and somehow he couldn't bear to just leave her where she'd died. Her brown leather collar still had her name tag and NARPAC registration disc with the blue cross on the front attached to it. A dog that was registered wouldn't be put down as an unwanted stray. Her official registration number was written on the the back along with: FINDER PLEASE REPORT THIS NUMBER TO NEAREST NATIONAL ANIMAL GUARD.

He took Misty's collar off her neck as carefully as if she'd still been alive and slipped it into his pocket. Then he wrapped her body in some sacking and laid it in a hole that had been left when the work on the station had stopped, leaving many tunnels unfinished and piles of rubble lying about. He covered the hole with bricks and pieces of cement and stood looking at it for some time.

He wished he'd been able to do as much for his fellow soldiers who'd been lost at Dunkirk. The cries of the dying men haunted him whenever he closed his eyes and tried to sleep.

Daniel swallowed hard as he remembered. He'd

never forget their faces. But now he had the mother of the pups to attend to. He found two sticks and tied them together to make a cross for Misty's rough rubble grave.

'Rest in peace,' he said. His voice felt hoarse from lack of use. 'Rest in peace.'

Chapter 10

When Amy got home from another day of helping Ellie with the dog-training classes, she found her mum holding a telegram and looking upset.

'It's your grandpa . . .'

'Oh no!' Amy cried, fearing the worst.

'His house has been bombed and we need to go and fetch him and bring him back home with us.'

'But what if he doesn't want to come?' said Amy.

She remembered how her grandpa had insisted that he wanted to remain in his own home when they'd invited him to stay with them before.

'I don't think he'll have any choice now,' Mrs Dolan said sadly.

They caught the train and then a bus to Woolwich. On the way Amy told her mother more about Michael's search-and-rescue missions and the kitten he'd recently found.

'Michael is only a year older than me,' Amy said with admiration.

But Mrs Dolan was horrified at the idea that Amy might want to do the same thing, and told her so.

'I don't want you even thinking of doing something like that,' she said.

'But I want to help . . .'

'Then find a safer way to do it. Dog-training classes are one thing, but bomb sites are quite another!'

Amy opened her mouth to say that Michael was only allowed into buildings that had been checked by an ARP warden first, but decided now was not the time. Her eyes filled with tears as she stared out of the window. She wasn't used to her mother being so sharp with her. But then she remembered what Jack had said about people sounding mean when they were scared. And her mum was scared. Everyone was scared.

Over in South London there were so many potholes in the bomb-struck roads that the red double-decker bus had to swerve and roll to avoid them. Amy looked out of the bus window to try and distract herself from worrying about her grandpa.

None of the houses seemed to have been left with their windows intact, and many also had missing front doors from the force of the blasts. Everywhere people were clearing up as best they could, just like they'd been doing in Swan Street where she lived.

Sometimes the bombs had destroyed a few

houses in a row; at other times only one or two seemed to have been struck. It was like a bizarre game of chance, only it was your home and everything you'd known could be lost or saved in an instant.

'Mum . . .'

Mrs Dolan saw the worry on Amy's face at seeing so many bombed streets from the bus window.

'Let's walk the rest of the way,' she said, trying to distract Amy.

But a few minutes later, as they turned the corner to her grandpa's street, Amy gasped. The gas main was blazing and fire engines all around were trying to put it out. Huge hoses criss-crossed the road and the acrid smell of smoke was everywhere as people shifted through the rubble with a sense of utter despair. None of the houses in her grandfather's street were still standing. Sewage seeped into the street from a shattered pipe.

'Stay close, Amy,' Mrs Dolan told her, taking her hand. There was no point going any further. Amy's grandpa's house was totally destroyed.

They found him in the local primary school. The Women's Voluntary Service had turned the school into a rest centre for people who'd been made homeless by the bombing.

'Bombees?' a woman from the WVS asked Amy and her mother cheerily as they arrived.

'Beg pardon?' said Mrs Dolan.

'Bombees? Have you been bombed out of your home?'

'Oh no, we've come over from North London,' Mrs Dolan told her.

'We've come to fetch my grandpa,' explained Amy.

The old man was sitting in a child's chair that was too small for him with a blanket round his shoulders, looking very sorry for himself.

'Dad,' said Mrs Dolan.

He looked up at her with red, watery eyes and for a moment or two it seemed he had no idea who she was.

'Forty years I lived there,' he said. 'Forty years and now it's gone.'

A WVS woman brought him a cup of tea, but his hand shook so much that a lot of it spilt.

'We're going to take you home with us, Dad,' Mrs Dolan said.

'Forty years . . .'

'You'll be safer.'

'Forty years . . .' Tears ran in rivulets down his face. 'I don't want to leave my home.'

But he didn't have a home any more.

Once they got back to Amy's house, Mrs Dolan took the old man's bag, with the few belongings he'd managed to salvage, up to Jack's room where he'd be sleeping from now on.

'Where's Misty?' Grandpa asked Amy.

'She's lost,' Amy told him. 'She ran away when the bombing started.'

'Poor little thing,' her grandpa said. 'Must be scared out of her wits.' Amy's grandpa was a dog lover like Amy.

'I'm helping my friends train other dogs so that they know what to do in the bombings, and can even help with search-and-rescue missions. We want them to set up another national War Dog Training School,' Amy explained.

'They used trained dogs like that a lot as messenger and guard dogs in the last war, you know,' the old man told her. 'Some even brought first aid to wounded soldiers. I think it'd be a fine idea to set up another school.'

When Mr Dolan came home, he told them how people had been coming into the Underground station, where he worked, all day long and buying penny tickets, but not using them.

'Wise souls,' Amy's grandpa said and Mr Dolan raised an eyebrow.

'They'll be wanting somewhere safe to shelter if there's more bombs tonight,' he said. 'And there's naught safer than the Underground. That's where we went in the Great War. Safe as houses down there, much safer than houses to be honest!'

'Can't be very comfortable,' Mrs Dolan

said. Although the truth was they weren't very comfortable in the Anderson shelter either.

'No, but you'd be safe,' Grandpa said and Mr Dolan nodded.

Mrs Dolan set about making a flask of tea and some sandwiches and Mr Dolan brought down the cardboard suitcases they used when they went on holiday to put their blankets and pillows in.

No one wanted there to be any more bombs that night, but if there were they'd be ready. An hour later the air-raid siren went off. There wasn't time to get to Wood Green Station so they hurried to the Anderson shelter. But, once the all-clear sounded, they headed for the station.

'All right, Jim?' Mr Dolan's fellow station clerks greeted him and he nodded. They went down the steps to the platform that was already crowded with people – many of whom they knew.

Mrs Dolan laid out their bedding and looked enviously at the people who'd brought portable mattresses with them. Her hip wasn't going to like lying on the hard concrete floor at all. But at least it was warm down here, unlike the Anderson shelter, almost too warm.

'Night night,' Amy's grandpa said and a moment later he was sleeping like a baby, while all around him other people chatted and played cards and knitted and laughed.

There was a strong sense of camaraderie among

the Londoners: a camaraderie that had only been strengthened by the bombing. They wouldn't be beaten by a bully they told each other, no matter how many bombs he dropped on them.

Chapter 11

When Bark and Howl awoke, they found Sheba beside them with another rat offering. After they'd eaten, Sheba taught them the art of keeping very, very still and waiting patiently until the rats thought they were safe and almost came to them before they pounced.

For a long time it seemed like it was going to be too much for the puppies. The sight of the rats was too exciting. Their natural inclination was to bound after them. But that usually meant they spent a lot of time running about with their tails wagging excitedly and very little time actually catching any food. Their squat little puppy legs weren't designed for speed, and to successfully catch rats they needed guile too – and that could only come with experience.

At last, Bark managed to stay still long enough and was rewarded with a tasty rat; then Howl managed it too. Rats were easily fooled by them when they stayed motionless, but skittered away fast as soon as they moved.

Sheba also taught them to hunt as a team, corralling the rats to trap them. The first few times they tried this Bark and Howl moved too swiftly and the rats escaped, and when a confused rat raced towards Howl by mistake he was so surprised he jumped back and the rat ran on past him to safety.

As the weeks passed, Bark and Howl grew used to their new life without their mum. They never forgot her though, and would often wake up whimpering for her. Then Sheba would lick them with her rough cat tongue that tickled much more than their mum's soft, comforting tongue ever did, and soon they'd be playing again.

For Bark and Howl, a toy could be anything from a piece of string to a pigeon feather. When Howl found a broken, discarded shoe, he clamped on to it with his sharp puppy teeth, shaking it for all he was worth, making little growling sounds as he subdued the ferocious shoe beast.

When Bark saw the new toy, he wanted to play too and grabbed the other end of it, and soon the puppies were in the middle of their first tug of war. First Bark took the lead and dragged Howl down the access tunnel, then Howl pulled him back the other way. They yipped and yapped with excitement as they lost themselves in the game, completely unaware that they were being watched.

Stanley had sold newspapers outside Wood Green Underground Station for more than fifty years. All day and long into the night, in all weathers, he stood in his box and called out to passers-by: 'Read all about it! Read all about it!' But nowadays the cold winds and frosty mornings wormed their way into his old bones and stayed with him all day, and this December it seemed worse than ever. He longed for the sun and an easy chair and a bucket of hot water to soak his feet in, but most of all he longed for the bombs to stop so he could get a good night's sleep.

The morning of Christmas Eve was bitterly cold and Stanley slipped inside the station to get a bit of warmth. As he was blowing on his frozen fingers, he heard the yips and yaps of puppies playing. It was a sound he hadn't heard since he was a boy.

Stanley groaned as he crouched down and looked through a broken grating, a smile spreading over his wrinkled face. Two puppies, who couldn't have been more than three months old, pounced on an old shoe and rolled around on the ground, trying to take it from each other before one or other of them got it and ran off with it with the other chasing him.

The sound of a train whistle startled them both and the first puppy suddenly let go of the shoe to join in with a howl. The second, who'd been pulling the shoe as hard as he could, suddenly had nothing to hold him and flew backwards, landing on the ground with a bump and a look of surprise on his face.

Stanley couldn't stop himself from laughing out loud. The puppies stopped playing and froze and Stanley clamped his mouth shut. He should have remembered that a dog's hearing is much better than a human's. He held his breath and waited.

A few seconds later Bark put his paw out to Howl and they were off again.

Stanley stood stiffly back up. Those newspapers weren't going to sell themselves. His eyesight might be good, but his knees felt every single one of his seventy-three years. As he stretched, he noticed a cat watching him.

'Hello, puss,' he said.

It was an old, scrawny-looking cat with one ear missing. Been in more than a few fights by the look of it.

'Puss, puss.' He held out his hand.

But the cat didn't come to him. Ragged tail held high, Sheba stalked away.

Stanley shook his head and laughed out loud. 'My hand not good enough to stroke your royal fur then?' he called after her.

He went back out into the cold again: 'Read all about it! Read all about it!' he shouted to passers-by.

Most of the news was the war of course, and the nightly bombing raids that had started in September and hadn't stopped ever since, not even once.

It was mid-morning when Mr Ward walked past Stanley on his way into the station.

'Oh good, you're here,' Stanley said, seeing his NARPAC uniform.

'Can I help you?' Mr Ward asked him, slightly bemused.

'Underground's no place for puppies to be playing,' said Stanley.

'Are there puppies here?'

'Yes, I thought that's why you'd come,' Stanley said.

Mr Ward shook his head. He'd been called in by the station staff, but not about puppies. There was a pack of feral dogs that were making a nuisance of themselves at the entrance to the station and there had been complaints. It had started with just three or so at first, but with winter coming the number had gradually increased, and now the stationmaster wanted the dogs gone.

'Those puppies can only be a few months old,' Stanley said.

'I'll see that they're removed too,' said Mr Ward. Puppies were just one of the consequences of having a pack of feral dogs in residence.

'I'd take one myself, only . . .' Stanley shrugged. 'The war and all . . .'

Mr Ward nodded and went into the station where he was met by the stationmaster who was very concerned about the pack of feral dogs.

'They could cause an accident on the road and they're a health hazard at the very least, and what if one of them bit someone? What sort of Christmas present would that be?' the man said.

'So they've actually been going up to people?' Mr Ward asked him.

'No,' he admitted. 'But I've no doubt they will soon. Better to sort them out before an incident occurs.'

Mr Ward went round to the back of the station, where the dogs were often to be found, to see for himself. He saw the rump of one dog as it slept by a pig bin and the skinny body of another that slunk away at the sight of him. He didn't see any puppies.

Mr Ward sighed. It wasn't the dogs' fault, but the stationmaster was right. They could easily prove to be a nuisance especially as it got colder and their pack size increased. Mr Ward told him the pack would be removed that afternoon.

'Couldn't be soon enough for me,' the stationmaster said. 'Nasty brutes!'

Sheba didn't trust the pack of feral dogs either; she remembered the dog who'd tried to attack Misty at the pig bins. Sheba tried to keep the inquisitive puppies away from the pack that now lived on the other side of the station. Bark and Howl, snuggled up together, could heard them at night, growling and barking and fighting.

Chapter 12

The NARPAC team wore thick protective gloves and carried dog-catching sticks with wire hoops on the end. No one expected the feral dogs to leave the station area willingly. Mr Ward supervised the three-man team and Michael went with him.

The first problem they faced was that there were even more dogs than Mr Ward had originally thought. Second was the fact that now the stationmaster wanted not only the dogs but the feral cats removed as well. Everyone knew cats were even harder to catch!

The leader of the feral dog pack was a German shepherd who'd once been a guard dog, until her owner had gone off to war, leaving the dog to fend for herself as best she could.

Life as a guard dog had been tough and so life as a feral dog suited her. She didn't want to be removed from her new home and she certainly didn't want a man from NARPAC putting a wire hoop round her neck. Mr Ward was sweating from the effort of trying to catch her.

Bark and Howl had heard the commotion through the tunnels and came to see what the fuss was about. Bark put his nose to the grill bars of the ventilation tunnel and peered out.

He watched as the German shepherd turned and ran along the length of the platform and Mr Ward ran after her and cornered her. She turned and bared her teeth at him and growled, then lunged towards him, barking as Mr Ward effectively lassoed her with the hoop on the end of the stick. Now the German shepherd really didn't stand a chance of escaping.

Bark was so busy watching the big dog and the man that Michael managed to grab him before he even realized what was happening.

'Got you.'

Bark struggled and squirmed and nipped at him. It was the first time he'd ever been touched by a person and he didn't like it. But Michael didn't let go. He held the puppy to him. Its heart was beating very fast and it was obviously terrified.

'Hush now,' he said soothingly. 'Hush now, you're OK.'

But Bark didn't want to be soothed and he wriggled desperately to get free. From the shadows

Howl watched. Sheba had taught him the art of waiting silently and now he did so, although all he wanted to do was run and bark at the human who had his brother.

Michael watched through the grill as more dogs from the feral pack came running along the platform, led by a great slavering brute of a dog. More men from NARPAC ran after them and tried to round them up. The leader, crazed and determined not to be taken, bit out at the dog poles and at the men holding them. But it was a hopeless battle that he couldn't win as more of the pack were taken to the dog van and more men were left free to try and catch him.

As he clasped the puppy to him, Michael knew he couldn't hand it over. What chance would it have in a pack like that? And the chances of anyone adopting it, adorable as it might be, were practically nil. No one had the time to take on a puppy during wartime, not when folks didn't know what tomorrow might bring or even if they'd have a home to go to.

He couldn't let the puppy go with the other dogs to the animal shelter. And he wouldn't.

Bark whined and Michael heard a faint whimper in response. So there was more than one puppy!

He didn't relax his hold on Bark, but slowly reached into his pocket and pulled out some dog biscuits. He gave one to Bark and scattered the others across the ground far enough away from him that a hungry puppy wouldn't be too scared to take them.

For Howl the smell of the dog biscuits was almost irresistible. Michael was turned away from him and seemed to be paying him no attention at all. Howl raced forward, grabbed a dog biscuit, gulped it down and raced back into the shadows. Michael didn't even seem to notice he was there and there were more biscuits on the ground. More biscuits waiting for Howl to crunch.

He crept forward, braver this time, coming closer to Michael, almost within reach of his hand, but, just as Michael was about to try and grab the second puppy, Bark yapped a warning and Howl skittered away as Bark struggled to escape too.

'Oh no you don't,' Michael said, holding the wriggling puppy more firmly. 'You're coming with me.'

He watched as his father came on to the platform. Michael was still hidden behind the grill and so Mr Ward couldn't see him and had no idea where he was.

'Michael, we're heading back,' he called out. 'There's supposed to be two puppies, but we can't find them. Must have moved on.' Then Michael heard him mutter, 'Where is he?'

'OK, Dad, I'll see you back at home,' Michael

called and grinned as the older man looked round, but still didn't spot him.

'I'm taking Sky to Ellie's training class,' Mr Ward called out. Now not only was Ellie running the general dog-training classes, but she was training the dogs for their search-and-rescue missions too.

Usually Michael would have wanted to go with him. There was a lot of work involved. But he couldn't go today. At least Ellie should have Amy there to help her.

'OK, see you later.'

The puppy wriggled in his arms, but this time Michael didn't speak. Another NARPAC official called Soames had come on to the platform to join Mr Ward.

'Rough pack,' Soames said. 'And not a collar or ID tag among the lot of them.'

'Rum times,' said Mr Ward.

'I thought that big mutt was going to have my finger off,' Soames said ruefully. 'Shan't be sorry to see him go.'

Michael knew what the fate of the feral dogs would most likely be – death. The sad reality was there were just too many stray dogs and not much chance of them being rehomed during wartime. He didn't want the puppy to be put down. He could not let that happen.

If only he could get the other puppy too. It was still there, hidden in the shadows. But it would be hard to keep hold of two wriggling, biting puppies. Maybe it'd be best to smuggle them home with him one at a time.

Michael didn't really like leaving the second puppy, but if someone from NARPAC saw him with them both there'd be questions asked. He didn't want his father to be in trouble and he didn't want to be forbidden from helping with the rescue missions.

The Underground grew quieter and Michael left with Bark, whom he'd named Henry, hidden under his coat.

'All right, lad? The rest of them have already gone,' Stanley, in his newspaper box at the entrance to the Underground, said when he saw him. Michael hurried on.

As soon as Howl realized Bark was being taken away, he ran after him through the Underground station, unseen. Every now and again worried whimpers came from him unbidden.

He gave a single bark from the entrance to the ventilation tunnel. But Bark didn't come back and Howl wasn't brave enough to leave the only home he'd ever known and follow them outside.

Head hanging low, Howl made his way back, barely aware of his surroundings. They'd been together for almost every moment of his whole life and he'd never been without his brother before.

Suddenly, from the shadows, there came a low,

menacing growl. Howl jumped and looked up to find himself staring into the great muzzle of the feral dog that had tried to attack them at the pig bin. The dog's eyes were crazed, drool dripped from his mouth as his growl grew louder. His lips curled back to reveal a set of razor-sharp teeth. Howl looked around and would have run, but the huge dog was blocking his path.

Most older dogs don't attack puppies, but Howl knew this dog was different. And, now that he had escaped from the NARPAC team, the great beast was clearly frightened, angry and desperate – a very dangerous combination. He wanted to attack the men who'd trapped him and tried to force him into the van – but they weren't here and Howl was.

His hackles were raised and he loomed over the puppy aggressively. Howl crouched low, his tail tucked in and his ears flattened in a submissive pose. He offered his paw to try and placate the much larger dog, but it didn't work. Howl's heart was beating very fast and he gave an involuntary cry of terror as the big dog crouched down, ready to pounce.

Howl was less than half the other dog's weight and had only ever play-fought with his brother before. He flipped on to his back, showing his tummy, another show of submission to the great hound and a final attempt to stop the attack. But it was no good. A second later the older dog sprang at Howl, teeth bared.

Howl yelped as the much larger dog's teeth sank into his tender puppy flesh. Before Howl could wriggle free, the larger dog clamped his jaws round Howl's little throat, going in for the kill.

Just at that moment, both dog and puppy were startled by a high-pitched yowl that echoed down the tunnel. Sheba had heard Howl's cry. At the sight of one of her puppies being attacked she now hurled herself on the back of the huge dog, who released Howl in surprise. The vicious dog spun round, trying to remove Sheba from his back. But Sheba clung on and dug her sharp claws through his fur and into his skin.

She didn't let go as the dog reared and shook himself vigorously. She clung on, knowing instinctively that if the dog removed her from his back she'd become his next victim, and she had to protect her puppy.

As he bucked and reeled in pain, the dog and cat came out of the hidden tunnel and on to the platform.

'What in the world . . .?' one of the station-cleaning crew said. He started to go towards the dog and its cat rider, but saw the dog's slavering jaws and thought better of it. He'd assumed the men from NARPAC had taken all the dogs, but they'd obviously missed this one.

He blew his whistle sharply instead, and for a split second the cat and dog froze at the shrill sound. But then the dog clamped his teeth round Sheba's left front leg and she let out a howl of pain as the bones gave way. Her right paw raked across the dog's eyes and temporarily blinded him so that he fell over the side of the platform on to the rails.

The station cleaner yelled, 'Look out!' but it was too late and there was nothing he could do to stop the emergency train as it raced along the rails, not stopping at the station. The dog didn't stand a chance.

The shocked station cleaner sighed, breaking the silence, and went to alert the stationmaster before another train came through.

From the platform there came a quiet cry. Sheba had been thrown from the dog's back, moments before he fell on to the tracks. Bleeding heavily, she slowly dragged herself on her stomach to Howl who was shaking and whimpering in the ventilation tunnel. He nuzzled his face to hers and she licked his head and purred softly to him. Then she closed her eyes and didn't open them again.

Howl lay beside Sheba's still body. He too was bloodied and battered; his breathing faint, he slipped into unconsciousness and didn't stir as hands lifted his limp body and carried him away.

Chapter 13

Michael tried to smuggle Henry into the house and up to his room, although he wasn't exactly sure what he was going to do with him then.

He should have realized his plan could never work. The other pets in the house immediately alerted Michael's mother to the fact that something was going on. Heggerty barked and wagged her tail. The cats circled round the lump under Michael's coat and even the kitten they'd recently rescued came to see what was going on.

'Mummy's *po-ppet*, Mummy's *po-ppet*,' the parrot squawked.

Michael sighed as Henry peeked out of his coat. 'I should have known,' he said.

'What's all that racket for?' Mrs Ward said suspiciously, and then she gasped as she saw the puppy's little face.

'I'm calling him Henry,' said Michael, already prepared that he might have to fight to be allowed to keep him. Only the day before they'd turned a lady away who wanted them to care for her cat. They just didn't have room for any more animals.

'I'm sorry, but we can't squeeze so much as another guinea pig in,' Mr Ward had said, closing the door on the distraught woman.

They all found it very difficult to turn any animal away, but they had no choice. Their home and garden were full to overflowing. To keep taking in more and more pets would mean they couldn't properly take care of those they already had.

Now Michael dreaded his mother telling him he couldn't keep the puppy.

'Oh, aren't you adorable?' Mrs Ward said, taking Henry into her arms. Henry nuzzled his head into her neck. 'Are you hungry? I bet you're hungry, poor little thing.'

'Have a carrot, have a carrot,' squawked the parrot as Mrs Ward disappeared with Henry into the kitchen.

Michael sighed. Henry was his puppy. He was the one who should be feeding him. He followed them into the kitchen where he found Henry lapping greedily at a bowl of cold porridge.

'Puppies are always hungry,' Mrs Ward smiled and Michael grinned. At least his mother was clearly smitten and would probably let him keep Henry. He didn't imagine for one second that his father would be as easy to persuade.

Henry finished the porridge and started sniffing around the kitchen. Michael thought he was looking for more food, but Mrs Ward didn't agree.

'Quick, take him outside,' she said, giving Michael a push towards the puppy. Michael grabbed him as Mrs Ward opened the back door.

'Doesn't take long for food to go through them at this age,' she said.

And she was right. No sooner had Michael put Henry down than he'd done his business.

Michael thought of the other puppy, the one he'd had to leave behind.

'There were two of them,' he said.

'So where's the other one?' Mrs Ward asked him.

'Still there – I hope,' said Michael.

'Oh, Michael,' Mrs Ward said. 'The poor little thing. You'll have to go back for it. I'll watch this one.'

Michael nodded and took a few pieces of yesterday's chicken with him to tempt the puppy out from the shadows at the station.

Mrs Ward stroked Henry's little furry head and Henry soon found that he didn't mind being stroked at all. When she stopped, he pushed his head under her hand for more.

'Back already?' Stanley the newspaper seller said when he saw Michael.

As he wasn't officially part of NARPAC this time

and didn't want to be noticed, Michael bought a ticket and headed down the steps like any other passenger, before ducking into the disused tunnel where he had found Henry.

He pulled the chicken from his pocket and waved it in the air, hoping the puppy would find it too much to resist.

'Puppy, puppy, here, boy,' he called. But no puppy came.

He stepped in something sticky and when he looked down he realized it was blood. A lot of blood. Could the puppy have been injured?

He hurried out on to the nearest platform. A station cleaner was down on the rails.

'Have you seen a puppy?' Michael asked him.

'Pets aren't allowed on the Underground,' the man said. 'It's expressly forbidden. There's signs up saying so. Not that I've yet come across an animal that could read.'

'He might be injured.'

The station cleaner told Michael about the dog that had died on the track.

'Wouldn't have called that dog a puppy though. Too big and aggressive.'

Michael went back to where he'd first seen the blood. He tried to follow the trail, but it led nowhere. Perhaps the other puppy had been scared by the accident and run away. Michael finally gave up looking and went home, but he resolved to tell

Amy about the second puppy so they could both keep a lookout.

Henry raced to him as soon as he walked through the door and licked and licked his face. Michael sat down and lifted him on to his lap, but he couldn't help feeling sad about the other puppy.

'That puppy's beautiful,' Mrs Ward said, coming into the hallway, 'but he's pongy.'

'We'd be pongy too if we'd lived our whole lives in the Underground,' said Michael, laughing.

They went into the kitchen and filled a tin bath with warm water before carrying it outside. 'Don't think Henry's going to like this much,' said Michael and he was right.

If Henry had been asked, he'd have told him that water and Henry weren't supposed to meet. They never had before, but Heggerty was there too and Michael was tempting Henry with pieces of chicken that smelt so good. He went a few steps forward and when Michael lifted him up he didn't struggle, but when Michael gently lowered him into the bath he did – a lot! Michael held on and soon, between him and his mother, Henry was soaking wet and soapy and then rinsed and clean.

Mrs Ward lifted him out with a big towel and wrapped it round him.

'Oh no you don't,' she said as he tried to wriggle out of it. She didn't want him drying himself by running round the garden and rolling in the flower beds.

She gave the pup to Michael and he carried him back inside and set about rubbing him dry while Heggerty sat close by and watched. Henry liked the feel of the towel stroking him. He stretched up his neck so Michael didn't forget to dry underneath his chin.

Once Henry was fairly dry, Michael set about brushing him before his dad and Sky came home.

'We're going to make you irresistible so he'll have to let you stay,' Michael told Henry as he brushed his fur until it shone.

Mrs Ward and Michael exchanged a look. They both knew it might not be enough that Henry looked adorable. They simply didn't have room for any more pets.

By the time Mr Ward and Sky came home an hour later Henry looked quite different to the puppy Michael had smuggled out of the Underground, and he smelt a lot sweeter too!

'We're back!' Mr Ward called out. 'Ellie's put us all through our paces and if Lieutenant Colonel Richardson isn't impressed – well, he should be. Ellie and Amy have been working like troopers.'

Michael wished he could have been at the class to help them, but Henry needed him more. He wished he could have found the other puppy too.

Sky raced into the kitchen and Henry fell totally and instantly in love with her. His tail wagged so hard it looked like it was going to fall off. He nuzzled his face to hers, barked and did a play bow to her before finally rolling on his back to show her his soft puppy tummy.

'Who's this?' said Mr Ward.

'Isn't he a poppet?' Mrs Ward said, winking at Michael.

'He is indeed, but where did he come from?' Mr Ward asked. He sat down and patted his knees so that Henry went to him. 'I see he doesn't have a collar, but he looks too well cared for to be a stray – although he is on the thin side.'

Michael had never been able to lie to his dad and very soon the whole story came out. And all the time it was being told Henry sat in front of Mr Ward with one ear up and one ear down as if he were listening too. Mr Ward wasn't pleased when he heard where the puppy had come from.

'You can't just take your pick of a pack of feral dogs.'

'He wasn't part of the pack. There were two puppies. I don't know where the mum was, but they weren't even in the same part of the station as the rest of them. They were on their own.'

'And what happened to the other puppy?' Mr Ward asked. 'Where's he?'

'I don't know,' Michael admitted. 'I went back

to look, but there wasn't any sight or sound of him when I called.'

'You know you shouldn't . . .'

Michael nodded. He knew. 'But what would've happened if I'd let them take him?' he said.

His father and he both knew only too well what had happened to hundreds of thousands of pets at the start of the war.

'What's going to happen to the others – those that have been taken back to the shelter?'

They both knew no one was going to claim any of them. None of the dogs, as far as they could see, had had a collar with an identification tag on it.

Michael pressed his face against Henry's soft puppy fur. 'They'll just be destroyed.'

'Not necessarily,' said Mr Ward and he told Michael about the directive they'd just received. 'Any stray dogs that have the potential to help with the war effort are to be assessed.'

There was a chance, albeit a slim one, that one of the dogs from the station might pass the assessment.

Henry pounced on Mr Ward's shoelaces and tugged at them as if they were worms.

'We'll have none of that, thank you,' Mr Ward said firmly, but his eyes were smiling.

Henry sat back and looked at Mr Ward consideringly, his head to one side, as if he understood every word that was said and was taking it all in. Mr Ward laughed and Michael knew

Henry wasn't going to be heading for the animal shelter that night.

'It's Christmas Eve, Dad,' said Michael.

Mr Ward looked over at his wife and he could see she was almost as desperate to keep the pup as their son was. It was hopeless. He'd said no more animals and they didn't have room for a pup.

'Just over Christmas,' he said sternly, and missed the look that passed between mother and son because the parrot started squawking, 'Merry Christmas, *me . . . rry* Christmas,' as it lifted one leg and then the other off its perch in a pacing movement.

'Merry Christmas to you too,' Mr Ward told the bird.

Chapter 14

Howl was in a bad way. As badly injured as some of the soldiers Daniel had seen at Dunkirk. His breathing was shallow and ragged. In the windowless room Daniel tended to Howl's wounds as the puppy trembled and cried out, his paws scrabbling feebly as if he were begging Daniel to take the pain away.

'You'll be OK, Soldier, at ease now,' Daniel said.

He'd stayed out of the way during the whole feral dog round-up, not wanting to be seen by the men from NARPAC. But he hadn't realized they would try to take the puppies too and now one of them was missing and the cat that had looked after them was dead. He'd found Howl lying beside her and had buried her beside her friend, the mother dog.

He felt so guilty as he bathed Howl's wounds and bandaged him up as best he could with what he could find. If he'd known the pups were in danger, he'd have come out to try and help them, whatever the consequences.

'That's it,' he told Howl. 'Nearly done.'

He did his best, but his torn sacking bandages weren't very clean and he was worried that whatever he did it wouldn't be enough to save the pup's life.

He squeezed some water into the corner of Howl's mouth; just a little, so it wouldn't choke him.

'That's it, Little Soldier, easy does it.'

Then he lay down beside Howl so he'd be there if he should need anything and to soothe him when he cried out in pain. He didn't know if the puppy was going to live or die. Howl was in shock from all the blood he'd lost and he shivered and whimpered in delirium as he lay on the sacking in the windowless room.

Daniel stayed close.

'Hush, Soldier, hush now,' he told the puppy, thinking back to how he'd tried to comfort his fellow soldiers who'd been injured at the front, even when their injuries were so bad there was little chance of survival.

After five days of marching, they'd finally arrived at Dunkirk beach only to find there were hundreds of thousands of other British, French and Belgian soldiers there already.

A red-headed infantryman called Fletcher had

shown Daniel a photograph of the girl he was going to marry.

'She's called Mary – but she doesn't like it when I call her Mary, Mary, quite contrary,' Fletcher said with a grin as they sat together on the sand.

The rumour was that the German army would be there any day and Daniel could hear the drone of aircraft in the distance. But the allied soldiers were ready for a fight, whatever the outcome. Around Fletcher and Daniel men boasted bravely to each other, even though they knew the odds were against them.

'Just let them come.'

'They'll see how real men fight.'

'They won't know what hit them when I get my hands on them.'

But it wasn't the army they needed to worry about. The attack came from the air and they didn't stand a chance against the German planes. They had no anti-aircraft guns on the beach; soldiers ran out from their scant cover and shot desperately up at the sky with their rifles.

Daniel was still holding Mary's photograph when the planes came. One minute Fletcher had been living and breathing and the next second he lay dead beside him.

But he wasn't going to let Howl die. Daniel had seen enough death, more than anyone should have to.

'You hang on in there, Soldier,' he said as Howl whimpered in pain.

If the puppy could just make it through the night then there was hope.

A few yards away, out on the station platform, the first of the people seeking shelter were arriving for the night, but Daniel was too busy to notice or care.

'Keep clear of the edge,' the station staff warned them. They didn't want anyone to fall on to the track, full of Christmas merriment, to be hit by an early-morning Tube train.

Even though it was Christmas Eve, Amy was there as usual with her mother and father and Grandpa. She'd come straight to the station from tidying everything away after the dog-training class and demonstration practice.

She smiled when she saw the Christmas tree that was really a potted plant decorated with bits of coloured paper by her mother.

She wished Jack could be there with them too. She'd never had a Christmas without him before. And she'd had very few, that she could remember, without Misty either. She wasn't looking forward to this Christmas much, if she were honest, but she put a smile on her face and called 'Merry Christmas' back as people greeted her.

Most of the people wore home-made paper hats

and there was an air of festivity about the station in spite of the war.

A few hours later the Christmas spirit was in full swing as people sang carols and Christmas songs and danced. No one forgot England was at war and had been bombed every night since September, but that didn't mean they couldn't have fun too.

Amy watched as two little girls skipped back and forth along the platform, laughing together. A toddler sitting on his mother's lap sucked on a wooden peg doll while his mother darned socks and joined in with the singing.

What Amy would have liked more than anything as her Christmas present was to have found Misty and to have Jack back home again. But as each day had passed it seemed less and less likely that Misty would ever be found, and Jack wouldn't get leave for several months yet.

Everyone cheered when a Tube train with Women's Voluntary Service ladies serving tea and buns pulled into the station. It even had a Santa Claus onboard!

Soon everyone was joining in with a rousing chorus of 'Santa Claus is Comin' to Town' followed by 'Jingle Bells'. Amy joined in too.

Henry's first Christmas Eve was completely different to his brother's.

'If he's going to stay then he'll have to obey the house rules,' Mr Ward told Michael and Michael readily agreed. 'And the first thing you can do is house-train him,' his father continued as he saw Henry disappearing behind the sofa to do his business.

'Henry, no!' said Michael, but it was too late.

Although Misty had taught her puppies to only 'go' in one area of the station, they hadn't been house-trained for life with humans. Henry had never even been outside the station before Michael took him home, so the concept of going outside to do his business was completely new to him.

Fortunately though, there was Sky, and as soon as she saw what Henry had done she growled and snapped at him before pushing him outside, sending a far clearer message than any of the Wards could have done.

From then on, if Henry wasn't sure of anything, he always looked to Sky for help. Michael was sure Henry would be more than willing to learn anything at all if it meant he got to spend more time with her.

'Come on, Henry, let's play,' he said and Henry's tail wagged as Sky joined in too.

The first thing Michael taught Henry was to fetch a toy and bring it to him for a treat. Henry was very fond of treats and got the idea in no time at all. Michael then taught him basic obedience: to sit, stay and come when he was called. Henry was a quick learner.

'He's so smart!' Michael told his mother.

During his first few hours Henry also learnt that it was OK to chase after a ball, but not OK to chase after the chickens or goats, that guinea-pig food did not taste as nice as dog food and that Heggerty didn't want him sleeping in her bed.

'Here, Henry, you sleep here,' Michael told him, patting the bed he'd made from some old blankets that he'd put next to Sky's bed. 'Lie down, Sky.'

As soon as Sky lay down, Henry curled up in his own comfy bed, and soon fell fast asleep with his stomach full and a bowl of water close by in case he felt thirsty during the night.

He woke up a few hours later and whined for Howl. They'd never been apart before. He crawled into Sky's bed and curled up beside her. Sky licked his ear and soon the sound of the other animals sleeping had soothed Henry back to sleep.

Christmas morning at the Wards' house started early. As always, Sky woke up first and raced up the stairs, closely followed by Henry. She pushed the door of Michael's room open and then raced in and jumped on the bed and Henry tried unsuccessfully to jump on after her.

'Merry Christmas,' Michael said, rubbing the sleep from his eyes. He led them both back downstairs and let them out into the garden where Sky supervised Henry.

It was a crisp morning and his parents weren't awake yet, so as a special treat Michael took Henry and Sky to the larger park around Alexandra Palace for a walk, or in Henry's case a run. Every now and again Henry would race ahead and then run back to Michael and Sky as if urging them to go faster, and then he'd be off again.

The smell of the horses that had run on the Frying Pan racing track was intoxicating to Henry and he was unable to resist tasting the manure left by the horses that trained there. Fortunately Sky was less tempted and barked at Henry to tell him to stop.

'Henry, no!' Michael shouted.

Henry looked up, stopped for a second and then snuffled up as much as he could before Michael reached him. 'You bad dog!' Michael said, but he was also laughing. Henry was such a little greedy-guts!

'Come on,' he said and Henry gambolled along after him. 'And no licking me,' Michael warned him. Henry wagged his tail as they left.

Heggerty was still in her own bed when they came back in, snoring contentedly. Once she'd been an early riser, but now she preferred to stay in bed until she could smell her breakfast. But the other animals wanted theirs straight away so Michael started filling their bowls.

'Merry Christmas,' he said to the parrot, opening its cage door so it could fly around while he changed its water.

'Merry Christmas, merry Christmas,' the parrot squawked and flew over on to the curtain rail and then perched on top of the lampshade.

One of the cats watched him with interest, but the Wards made sure the parrot was never left alone with them when he was out of his cage. The parrot's sharp beak could probably give a cat's claws a run for their money – but not ten cats' claws!

They never let the guinea pigs out of their cages unless they were safely in their run outside. They would have been too much for the cats, and probably now Henry, to resist.

'This place is turning into our own family zoo,' Mr Ward said later. But Michael shook his head.

'I'm sure the animals in the zoo aren't as spoilt as the ones living here!'

Heggerty gave Michael's turkey sandwich a meaningful stare.

'Go on then,' he said, giving her the crust, which she wolfed down in a gulp before looking up hopefully for more.

Fortunately everyone who popped round was too

busy wishing each other merry Christmas to ask many questions about where the new puppy came from. There were so many strays wandering the streets, they just assumed Henry was another one. But Michael couldn't wait to introduce Henry to Ellie and Amy.

Down in the Underground station Daniel went to find some food for Howl in the pig bins. He took care not to be seen, although most of the staff were too busy eating their makeshift Christmas lunch to pay him much attention.

'That'll do him good,' Daniel muttered as he took some leftover porridge and scrambled eggs. The food hadn't been there long and shouldn't be too rich for the pup in his present condition.

The smell of the food made Howl's sensitive nose twitch when Daniel returned. It was the smell that he associated with his mother – not the rats he had lived on more recently, but the food he'd shared with his brother as a young pup.

'Slow down there, Soldier,' said Daniel as Howl gulped the food. He broke the bread into smaller bits and fed them to him slowly, then gave him some water to drink. Howl tried to stagger to his feet, but he wasn't strong enough yet and he whimpered in pain and lay back down again.

'Rest now,' Daniel said as he stroked him. 'Rest and recover.'

The sound of Daniel's voice soothed him and Howl was soon fast asleep again.

As it was Christmas Day, Daniel decided Soldier needed a present, but the only thing he had to give him was Misty's collar with the NARPAC ID tag on it. He laid it beside Howl for when he woke up later.

The puppy's sleep was marked by twitching and cries. Daniel stroked him to try and soothe him. He wondered if he were having a nightmare about the fight he looked like he'd been in. Did dogs dream? He'd never thought about it before. But this one certainly seemed to be doing so.

Daniel dreamt too, try as he might not to, and it was always the same dream. The soldiers were packed together on-board the boat like sardines, but no one complained. All they wanted was to get home. Despite being hungry and having had no sleep for days, plus being soaked by the rough sea spray, they were in fine spirits as they saw the huge white cliffs of Dover in the distance, and a cheer went up.

They were almost home. They were safe.

Then the plane had come and the boat had been hit and he'd never forgotten the screams of the men as the boat caught fire and some of them were thrown overboard and some jumped into the waves as the boat sank.

It was five hours before he'd been rescued and

he was one of very few who'd survived. Later, in hospital, when he was half-delirious, he heard the term 'shell shock' for the first time. The doctors told him he didn't have to fight any more, that he was released from service because of his condition. Still scared and confused, Daniel didn't know what this really meant.

After he'd left the hospital, he'd decided to give Fletcher's photograph back to Mary and tell her in person what had happened to him.

He knew that she might not even be aware that he'd died. Not everyone had come home yet. Some of the soldiers in France had been taken prisoner, others had been shot, and then there were those who'd stayed behind to stop the German panzers from reaching the beach. Soldiers who would never see home again, but would save the lives of hundreds of thousands of men.

He'd travelled up from the coast to London to give Mary the news.

'I'm so sorry,' he said as he handed the photograph back to her.

What he hadn't anticipated was her anger.

'Why couldn't you have died instead?' she'd shouted at him. 'Why couldn't it have been you?'

Her words had stayed with Daniel, haunting him ever since. After that, he didn't know what to do or where to go. He thought everyone would be angry with him, like Mary had been. So, eventually, he had found the perfect hiding place in the station, and that was where he had been living ever since, too scared to face anyone.

Chapter 15

Every morning and evening, and sometimes in between, Daniel checked on Howl's bite wounds and cleaned them as best he could. Fortunately the salt that had been delivered to melt the ice on the station steps was stored close to the pig bins, and he mixed that with water to bathe the wounds. For a while it looked like one of the bites, the deepest, was infected, but Daniel's continued attention and the salt water helped it to heal.

The first time Howl wagged his tail was the first time Daniel smiled in a long, long time. It had been so long that it felt strange to his face as the unused muscles were put back to use. During the weeks it took for Howl to heal, Daniel smiled a lot more and grew to love the dog. As for Howl, he adored Daniel.

Daniel's fear of leaving the station had gradually grown during the months he'd been there until it had become all-consuming. Now even the idea of setting foot outside left him shaking with fear. But he also knew it had to be done for Howl's sake. It was cruel for a dog to live its life inside.

Howl had been so brave and Daniel felt ashamed and guilty that he hadn't been there to protect him when he'd needed him. He should have come out earlier to see what was happening. But the barking and panic of the feral dogs and the shouting of the NARPAC men had made him hide away. He hadn't thought about the pups and how they might need him. All he'd thought about was his own fear.

As Daniel stroked Howl, he knew that more than anything he wanted to take the pup to the park and share his joy as his paws touched grass for the first time.

But for that to happen Daniel would need to get over his fear of going outside. In the early hours of the morning, when he was sure there was no one about to see him, he began to try.

The first time he attempted to step outside, past the pig bins to the cobblestoned area at the back of the station, he found his legs refused to move. He felt sick and shaky, but, with steely determination, he'd grabbed his right leg between his hands and forced it forward.

The next night he did the same thing, only once he'd forced his right leg to move he grabbed his left leg between his hands and forced that leg forward too. He'd barely taken a step, but a cold sweat ran down his forehead, neck and back. As he gritted his teeth and forced his leg forward, he fell and lay on the ground, staring up at the night sky. He'd come further than the two or three steps he'd intended, thanks to the fall. There was still a long way to go.

But, as Howl gradually grew stronger, Daniel's night walks grew longer and, by the time Howl was fit enough to go for his first walk outside, so was Daniel.

He clipped Misty's collar round Howl's neck and tied a length of string through the loop.

'In case of cars, Little Soldier. You don't want to get hit by a car; that'd be very painful indeed,' he told the dog.

Howl was used to being able to go where he wanted and had never had a lead put on him before. He tried to bite at it.

'No, Soldier.'

And scratch at it.

'Leave it be.'

Howl didn't like his new lead much; it didn't let him go where he wanted to go. But he did like Daniel, very much.

It was so early in the morning that it was still quite dark as they emerged from the back of the station into Hardy Passage. The air outside felt and smelt very different to what Howl was used to, and every lamp post he passed had myriad dog scents on it, so strong that it was almost overwhelming and he had to stop and sniff while Daniel urged him onwards.

'Come on, Soldier, we're going somewhere I think you'll like,' he said as they went through what was left of the gates of Lordship Rec. Most of the wrought iron had now been removed, ready to be melted down and used for the war effort.

Howl had never smelt grass before and this grass was frosty with dew.

'There you go,' Daniel said, untying the string.

At first, Howl didn't leave Daniel's side, scared of the unfamiliar new world they'd entered.

'Go on, Soldier,' Daniel urged him.

Still Howl stayed close. Until he saw a squirrel. The bushy tail was too much for him to resist and he went chasing after it and sat at the bottom of the tree and whined when the squirrel raced up into the safety of its branches.

'That's what squirrels are like,' Daniel told him. 'Tricky!'

Daniel moved on and Howl trotted along behind him, glancing back every now and again at the tree where the squirrel had gone. Then he spotted another squirrel on the grass in the distance and raced after it. He got closer and closer as Daniel held his breath. Then came to a sudden halt. Howl sat down as the squirrel ran up the trunk of a tree and disappeared into the branches.

Howl looked up at the squirrel, threw back his

head and howled with disappointment. Daniel smiled when he saw the pup up to his old tricks again.

Under the tree, hidden in the grass close to the trunk, Daniel saw a ball and picked it up. It reminded him of the time he'd found a ball of string and how much fun the two pups, and the cat, had had with it.

'Here, fetch,' said Daniel, and he threw the ball and Howl raced after it. Almost as much fun to chase as a squirrel and balls didn't run up trees!

He brought the ball back to Daniel in his mouth and Daniel threw it and Howl got to chase after it again. Howl would have happily played the game all day long, but Daniel was aware of the time ticking past.

'We'd better head back, Soldier,' he said at last.

People were walking through the park now and the working day was beginning. It was time for them to go back to not being seen, back to being hidden inside the Underground station.

Daniel didn't want to meet or speak to anyone. He wasn't just ashamed of being alive when braver soldiers, ones with families and people who needed them, had died. He also felt ashamed of being invalided out of the army. Although he knew the effect of shell shock was all too real, there were still those who thought of it as the coward's way out.

He pushed the string through the hoop of Howl's collar.

'This way, Soldier.'

Howl looked behind him as they went through the gates and Daniel knew he'd really have liked to stay longer.

'We'll be back tomorrow,' he said.

Daniel was as good as his word and the next day they went back to the park, where Howl found another ball, by the rose garden this time, and Daniel threw it for him.

As the days passed, part of the fun of going to the park for Howl was looking for balls that had been lost. For Daniel, who'd once been so terrified to go out, their early-morning walks were now the highlight of his day.

He'd helped to heal Howl's physical wounds, but in return Howl was helping to heal his mental scars. As each day passed, Daniel grew a little more confident and dared to hope that one day he might return to living a normal life, with Howl by his side. Maybe he'd even be able to help in the war again.

'Find it,' Daniel would say, and Howl would search through bushes and hedges and long grass, his tail wagging constantly, until he found a ball – or something else interesting.

'A mitten?' Daniel said, laughing, when Howl presented him with a muddy mitten instead of a ball. 'That's not for throwing.'

Howl dived back into the bush and came out with a broken umbrella instead.

'And that's not for throwing either!'

Whenever Howl did find a ball, Daniel always threw it for him and Howl loved to race after it while Daniel watched him run. Howl was very fast.

Daniel hadn't really thought about how Howl would react to his first view of the lake. Of course the pup had never seen a vast expanse of water before. Water was scarce down on the Underground and the most he'd probably seen before was in a bucket.

The first time they went near the lake Howl didn't even seem to notice it. The second time he looked at it, but stayed close to Daniel. The third time they went Howl spent a long time watching the ducks on the lake with his head cocked to one side. But the fourth time Howl raced to the side of the water with Daniel's voice ringing in his ears: 'Soldier, come back!'

And then he raced right in. It was the first time he had ever felt water on his fur and the shock of its cold wetness almost stopped him, but only for a second.

'Soldier, here boy, here!' Daniel called from the side of the lake, but Howl didn't return. He was having too much fun!

As the water grew deeper, the ducks got closer and, as the water became too deep for him to stand in, Howl's legs started to paddle and he was swimming.

Daniel breathed a sigh of relief as he watched him. He knew dogs were instinctively supposed to be able to swim, but he'd still been worried for Soldier as he raced into that water.

Howl paddled towards a duck and the duck quickly swam off in the opposite direction. He swam towards another duck only to have it quack at him and fly away.

Daniel watched the dog almost enviously. He never wanted to go in the sea again, but the water in the lake looked so inviting. The next moment he'd thrown off his outer clothes and was wading into the water. He gasped at the icy coldness of it. But it was nothing compared to the hours he'd spent waiting to be rescued in the English Channel off Dover.

Howl doggy-paddled over to him and they swam out to the ornamental island in the centre of the lake together. As they crawled on to the bank, Howl shook himself vigorously beside Daniel.

'Watch where you're shaking that water, Soldier,' Daniel shouted as he got splashed.

Howl just wagged his tail and Daniel laughed. Then Daniel remembered that people would be walking through the park soon, taking short cuts to work.

'Time we were heading home, Soldier,' he said

after they'd rested a little. They swam back to the edge of the lake and climbed out, once again disturbing the ducks, which quacked and squawked as they waddled and swam away at the sight of them. Daniel rubbed himself dry as best he could with his clothes while Howl shook himself vigorously again and then rolled over and over in the grass. It was a lot easier for dogs.

Howl raced over to Daniel, wagging his tail as if to say, 'That was fun, wasn't it?' Daniel laughed, something he seemed to be doing a lot more often since he and Howl had become friends.

Chapter 16

Like his brother, Henry's favourite place to visit was Lordship Rec. The Wards' suburban garden was small and he always had to stay on his lead when they were walking down the road, but at the park he could run and run and run until he could run no more. Plus, Lordship Rec had a million interesting smells to sniff at and dogs to play with and squirrels to chase, not to mention the ducks and swans on the lake – which unfortunately he was forbidden to go after.

He was very excited when Amy came round because often, when she did, he and Sky would get taken for a walk to look for someone called Misty.

He waited by the front door, his tail wagging happily, as his lead was clipped to his collar and Amy said the word he liked most of all: 'Walk.'

'Heggerty,' Michael called out. 'Heggerty, do you want to come for a walk?'

Amy went to find the yellow Labrador, but smiled when she saw the dog lying fast asleep in the two-tier Morrison shelter the Wards had recently been given. It looked like an oversized silver steel-framed dining table with mesh sides that could be opened and it took up most of the dining-room floor. Mr Ward had put Heggerty's bed inside it, so she'd be safe at night, and she usually had the soundest of sleeps – or at least it seemed so judging by her contented snoring.

They'd only had the shelter a few days as Morrison shelters hadn't been available at the start of the war. But Heggerty had already got used to it, and she took herself off to her bed in the Morrison shelter when she felt like a nap during the day.

The Anderson shelter, in the back garden, was now also the chicken coop and the goat house. They all went in it every night to sleep and so at the first sign of trouble the goats and chickens headed for the safety of their home – which also just happened to be bombproof!

As soon as Henry saw the direction they were going, he started pulling on his lead, urging Michael and Amy onwards. Why were they going so slowly? Didn't they know they were going to the best place ever? Why weren't they running down the road as Henry would have been doing if he didn't have the lead round his neck?

But Michael and Amy were too busy chatting about the War Dog demonstration to pay attention to Henry. Lieutenant Colonel Richardson had accepted Amy's invitation to come and see the work that the NARPAC search-and-rescue dogs were doing. Ellie had screamed and grabbed the letter when Amy told her.

'You actually wrote to Lieutenant Colonel Richardson? And he actually said he'd come?' she said in disbelief. 'If he gives the go-ahead, the War Dog Training School could really happen!'

'Ellie has it all planned out,' Amy told Michael. 'And she's been in touch with all the other NARPAC groups to let them know about it and invited anyone with a dog who's been part of a search-and-rescue mission to come along too.'

'Sounds like we're going to need more chairs,' said Michael.

But Amy was sure people wouldn't mind if they had to stand. 'It's for such a good cause.'

Henry panted as he strained against his lead.

'Slow down, Henry,' Michael told him. 'You don't want to strangle yourself!'

Henry looked over his shoulder at Michael and slowed down a little, but the smell of Lordship Rec got to be too much, and then another smell – an even better smell – reached him and he pulled even harder.

As Henry and Michael reached the front entrance of the park, Howl and Daniel were just leaving through a smaller gate at the side of the park that Daniel preferred to use.

The dogs could sense each other from across the park and were wildly excited. But Michael was busy chatting to Amy and told Henry to 'Calm down now', not noticing Daniel and Howl in the distance.

On the other side of the park Howl was almost yanking Daniel's arm off and then he started howling. But Daniel was eager to get back to the safety of the station and dragged Howl out of the park.

As Howl disappeared, Henry jumped up at Michael and Amy, biting on his lead.

'Henry, stop it!' Michael told Henry firmly.

'What's got into him?' Amy asked. She looked down at Sky who wasn't pulling in the slightest. 'Good girl, Sky.'

'This isn't like you at all,' Michael told Henry.

Howl whined as he looked back at the park. But Daniel wouldn't stop.

'Come on, Soldier,' he said.

Back in the park Henry's wildly wagging tail gradually slowed and then drooped and finally dropped. He looked up at Michael and then back at the place where Howl had been but was now gone from. He whined.

The sight and smell of Henry was almost too much for Howl to bear, and he desperately didn't want to be parted from his brother so soon.

He pulled back on his lead and pressed his

claws into the ground to try and stop Daniel from separating them. But Daniel was so much stronger than him and forced him onwards. They turned the corner and Howl couldn't see the park any more, but the smell of Henry was still in the air. And it was too much. As they crossed the road opposite the station, he pulled against his lead again and this time the frayed string broke and he was free and racing over the busy road and back the way they'd come.

'Soldier, stop!' Daniel shouted as the dog ran into the road and Daniel ran after him.

The driver of the red London bus slammed on his brakes, but it was too late. Daniel cried out in pain as he was knocked to the ground.

The driver was shaking as he climbed down from his bus in shock. Had he fallen asleep at the wheel? He'd been so tired. Everyone was so tired. He and his fellow bus drivers were determined to keep London moving. Most people didn't have cars and without public transport the city would come to a standstill. But just before the accident he'd been thinking how good it would feel to be tucked up in his bed, fast asleep. He didn't know if he'd closed his eyes for a moment – he couldn't be sure.

'He came from nowhere,' he said. 'Nowhere.'

Howl stood on the opposite side of the road and whimpered, his brother forgotten as a new smell overrode all others. The smell of Daniel's blood on the road.

Cars and bicycles stopped and people came running to help the man lying in the middle of the road, who looked like a tramp.

'What happened?' they asked each other.

'Just came out of nowhere.'

'First that dog and then him . . .'

'Drunk, do you think?' a butcher's errand boy said as he climbed off his bike and looked down at Daniel, lying crumpled in a heap.

Howl stood trembling and confused on the other side of the road, staring at Daniel lying still on the ground. Still trembling, he went to stand beside him. He sniffed at the blood. The butcher's boy kicked out at Howl and shouted at him, mistakenly thinking Howl was going to lick up the injured man's blood.

'Get out of it!'

Howl whimpered and skipped back out of the way of the boy's feet, but did not leave.

Then the ambulance arrived and Daniel was lifted on to a stretcher and put inside it as Howl took a step closer, but was brushed out of the way. He barked and whined as the doors closed and the ambulance drove off, bells clanging. He ran after it, not wanting to lose Daniel, until he could run no more. A car horn honked at him, and he narrowly avoided being hit himself, and still he ran on.

But the distance between him and the ambulance only increased until it was impossible for Howl to catch up. The ambulance disappeared into the distance and the dog threw back his head in total misery and uttered a long, sorrowful howl.

When it was dark, he returned along the roads he'd run down earlier after the ambulance. He headed back to the darkness of the hidden parts of the Underground alone, back to the only home he'd ever known.

The smell of Daniel was everywhere. Howl climbed on to the bedding Daniel used, wrapping himself in his scent, and went to sleep miserable and more alone than he had ever been.

Chapter 17

Some search-and-rescue dogs, like Grace and Sky, seemed to know almost instinctively what it was they were supposed to do on a rescue mission. But others needed a little more help.

Henry would have willingly gone with Sky and Michael on their rescue missions, but first he needed to be assessed by Ellie.

'Come on, Henry, come with me,' Ellie said, waggling a rope toy in front of him. Henry took one end in his teeth and they were soon having a gentle tug of war.

Ellie nodded to Amy in the corner and she dropped two dustbin lids on the floor with a loud clatter.

Henry looked over at where the sound came from, but almost immediately went back to playing with the rope toy.

Ellie gave a thumbs up to Michael. If Henry had been frightened by the loud noise, she'd have been concerned. A rescue dog needed to be able to concentrate on his work however many loud sounds there were going off around him.

Ellie threw a ball for Henry.

'Fetch!'

Henry raced after it as Ellie nodded to Amy in the corner again. This time she fired a noisy starting pistol. Once again Henry looked over, but it didn't stop him from picking up the ball and running back to Ellie with it. He dropped it at her feet and looked up at her hopefully, wagging his tail. Ellie laughed and threw the ball again.

She looked over at Michael as Henry ran across the hall after the ball. He was sitting on a chair at the side, watching Henry like an anxious parent. This time she put both her thumbs up. Henry had passed the first part of the assessment with flying colours.

But there were still more tests.

Michael had taught Henry how to sit and also how to wait until he was called, which Henry still found extremely difficult. He was so desperate to move he was quivering with the effort, but he managed to stay where he was for the minute or so he was asked to do so by Ellie. She expected him to last for much longer than a minute eventually, but that would come with practice.

'Just gradually increase the length of time he has to wait, but don't expect too much too quickly and don't worry if it increases and then goes back a step or two. It'll come,' she told Michael.

Michael nodded. 'We'll work on it.'

He knew that Henry needed to be able to wait when he was asked to do so because sometimes they might find themselves in a situation where he needed to keep still, like if there was an unexploded bomb. There might not be time to clip on Henry's lead, or he might need to stay on the other side of the road, so it was crucial that he learn to wait without question.

As well as 'sit', he had to learn 'down', where he lay down on command. Fortunately Michael and Henry had been practising for this day ever since Henry had come to live at the Wards' house. Michael had trained Henry in basic obedience, and now Ellie put him through his paces as Michael watched him and tried not to bite his fingernails too much.

When she'd seen enough, Ellie came over to Michael in his chair, all smiles.

'He's a fine dog,' she said.

Michael let out the breath he'd been holding and grinned from ear to ear.

'Come on, Henry,' said Ellie. 'You're not done yet.' It was time to see what he was like at agility. This wasn't strictly part of the assessment test, but Ellie thought Henry would enjoy it and she thought he might be good at it too. Henry definitely had some collie in his breeding line and collies were often particularly good at agility.

Ellie was right. Henry excelled at it and had no fear of crawling through a narrow tunnel to find Michael and a treat waiting for him.

'Good dog, Henry,' Ellie told him. 'Good dog.'

She came over to Michael with Henry, who was excited and ready to do more.

'He didn't mind going in that tunnel at all,' Michael said. He'd seen some dogs refuse to go down them.

'He's a real trooper,' said Ellie with a smile. 'Dogs can do rescue work equally well in the dark as in the daylight. They use their senses of smell and hearing to their fullest in the dark of course. One well-trained dog is equivalent to about twenty human searchers in good conditions and many more in poor ones.'

'So how far could a dog detect a scent?' Amy asked, coming to join them.

'It depends on the conditions,' said Ellie. 'And of course we're not in ideal conditions searching bombed houses, but if we were then a dog could pick up a human scent from about five hundred yards away.'

Amy was very impressed.

'Want to do some more, Henry?'

Henry wagged his tail and followed Ellie.

Plank walking, A-frame, jumps and soft tunnel work were next and Henry did them all with ease.

'Let's try him on the split kennel,' said Ellie.

Michael wasn't sure Henry was ready for that yet; hardly any of the dogs were happy doing it. But Michael did as he'd been asked and helped to set the equipment up.

'You call him,' Ellie said.

Amy held Henry until Michael called out: 'Henry, come!' and then she released him into the narrow tunnel, which split into two. Which one would lead him to Michael? Decision made, Henry squeezed his way into the dark tunnel and pushed open a flap at the end to reach a delighted and amazed Michael, waiting for him with treats and praise at the ready.

'Good dog, Henry. Good dog!' he said as Henry gave his face an excited lick. 'First time!' he said to Ellie.

Ellie nodded. 'He's certainly got a lot of potential,' she said.

'He could do that in the War Dog demonstration,' Amy suggested.

Once Henry had passed his assessment, he joined Ellie's regular training class, along with Michael.

Henry loved the classes and was usually waiting at the front door ten minutes before it was time for him and Michael, as well as Mr Ward and Sky, to leave.

One of the first things Henry needed to learn was to remain calm under fire, but this wasn't a problem for him. He'd spent his whole life in the Blitz in London with bombs falling all around him. It was what he was used to. He practised this with the others, then he progressed on to taking messages and finding fake bomb victims buried under fake rubble.

The training always focused round the same clear pattern: command, action and then reward.

At home Michael hid Henry's toys and then got him to find them, and when he did he was always given a treat. Henry loved playing hide-and-seek, and now this game proved an invaluable first step as he learnt to look for people and animals and let Michael know when he'd found them.

One of the dogs at the training class was a four-year-old, glossy-coated German shepherd bitch.

Her trainer, George, told Michael she'd come from Wood Green animal rescue centre and Michael realized she'd been the one of the feral dogs from the Underground.

'Turning out to be a fine search dog, aren't you?' George said as he petted her proudly. He'd named her Lily and she looked up at George adoringly and wagged her tail. She was obviously very happy with her new search-and-rescue dog life and quite different to the angry, violent dog she'd once been.

Henry sat in front of them, one ear up and one ear down, his head cocked to one side – ready to play whatever game they wanted him to play next.

'You dog's fast,' George said and Michael and Mr Ward nodded.

'He is that.'

Henry was one of the fastest dogs anyone had seen when it came to the obstacle course. He was smart too: he didn't need to be told over and over what to do; he picked it up in no time and often correctly guessed what Michael wanted him to do even before he'd asked him to do it.

'Could do with more like him,' said George.

And Michael told him how there'd been two puppies living in the station. It was a shame they hadn't been able to find the other puppy, as he or she would probably have had the same potential. But although Michael had looked, and Amy still looked when she went to the station at night, there'd been no sign of him. Just as there'd been no sign of Misty.

Ellie got Henry to practise his scent skills over and over – which Henry was more than happy to do because to him it was all just one giant game. And she also made sure Henry learnt how to indicate clearly to Michael if he detected a scent, by barking, and Michael was instructed on how to carry out searches safely using Henry so that neither of them got injured – hopefully. Cut paws were an almost unavoidable hazard as there was so much broken glass everywhere on the bomb sites.

The first rescue mission Henry was allowed to go on was a great success. He found a cat whose worried owner was delighted to have returned to her.

His second mission was even more successful: Michael had checked a badly bombed house over and decided there were no humans or animals trapped inside it. But Henry didn't agree and, even though he was sneezing and coughing from the dust, he kept running over to and barking at one particular spot.

'Henry, come on, let's go,' Michael called to him. There were more houses that needed searching.

But Henry wouldn't come. Michael was just about to clip on Henry's lead and force him to do as he was told when he heard a faint cry: 'Help! Help us!'

'OK, we're here, you'll be fine,' Michael called out.

Piece by piece, Michael removed bricks, wood and plaster. Mr Ward came to help him and under the rubble they found two small children.

Henry barked with delight and Michael stretched out a hand to help them out of the hole. They'd been protected from the rubble by the tin bath they were partially hidden under, but it had also become a trap as more and more debris from the bomb had covered it, making it almost impossible for them to get out from underneath.

At times, the hazards of entering bombed-out buildings were overwhelming and Michael was worried for Henry's safety with ruptured gas mains, burst pipes, broken glass and, worst of all, dust everywhere that made him sneeze. But they went out anyway, in all weathers and all conditions. Their job was vital.

Chapter 18

As more and more people used the Underground to shelter in each night, there was less and less room for everyone. Soon queues of people wanting tickets for the night began in the early afternoon.

Although Mr Dolan worked for the Underground, his family still needed a ticket to go down on to the platform. Usually Amy was sent to join the queue, to buy a ticket for the whole family and reserve a night-time space for them. The queue could be so long it went right round the station.

Spaces nearest the stairs were always busy with people coming and going and you were likely to get trodden on, so she didn't choose them. Spaces near the rails were dangerous, and too far away from the stairs meant it took ages getting out of the station in the morning – so she didn't choose those either.

One warm spring day, despite arriving at the station just after lunch to reserve her family a space, she found that their usual spot had already been taken.

The new place she chose for them to sleep was near a grill hole in the wall. She placed blankets and pillows round her so there'd be enough space and as she did so she had the odd feeling that she was being watched. She looked behind her, but the other families were busy selecting their own spots and not looking her way.

Amy glanced at the grill hole in the wall and was just in time to see a pair of brown eyes staring at her before whatever it was ran away.

She knew it was too big to be a rat – unless it was a giant-sized one which she certainly hoped it wasn't. But she thought it could be a cat. Every now and again there'd be one at the station, which the staff always shooed away if they saw it.

She stayed very still and waited and waited until she thought she was going to burst from keeping still for so long, and that was when she saw the watcher clearly for the first time, out of the corner of her eye.

It wasn't a cat. It was a skinny dog with one ear that went up and one ear that went down.

Amy felt a tingle of excitement. She was sure this dog must be the missing puppy who'd been with Henry when Michael caught him almost four months ago. This dog was really good at hiding!

Only Amy was confused because this dog had a collar with a NARPAC identification disc on it and Henry hadn't had one.

Amy knew she had to take things slowly and be careful not to frighten it. She opened the bag of sandwiches her mother had sent with her and quickly stuffed one through the grill hole. As soon as she got near the grill to put it in, the dog disappeared of course. But she'd expected that to happen. She didn't know for sure, but she hoped it was still there somewhere, hidden, but watching from the shadows.

Inside the grill hole tunnel Howl found the smell of bread and home-made blackberry jam irresistible. Gradually he edged closer, watchful, ready to run back in an instant without the food if need be, but wanting it so badly he was drooling.

On the platform Amy waited. She didn't look inside the grill immediately – although she was desperate to do so – because she didn't want to frighten the dog. Inside the tunnel Howl gulped down the sandwich and raced back into the shadows where he waited and watched.

Ten minutes later Amy couldn't resist peeping through the grill. The sandwich had gone! She took out another one and popped that through the grill too. The first had been jam and this one was dripping. Howl thought they were both delicious in the millisecond it took him to gulp the second one down.

Over the next few days Howl began to look out for Amy and made sure he was in the tunnel behind the grill hole when she came. He was always hungry and Amy's food tasted so good!

As he was eating, Amy poked her fingers through the grill.

'There's a good dog,' she said. 'What a good dog.'

Her voice was soft and soothing. Inside the small tunnel Howl wagged his tail and licked Amy's fingers, which smelt and tasted of bread and jam.

The next afternoon Howl watched and waited at the grill hole as Amy spread out her family's bedding, hoping for more dripping or jam sandwiches. In the grill tunnel he heard the bomb go off in the distance, but took no notice as it was such a familiar sound. Amy didn't hear it because the Underground muffled the noise so that a bomb going off in the distance was too soft for human ears to hear.

The young ticket clerk brought the people on the platform the news ten minutes later. Her face was grey with shock.

'Swan Street . . .'

'What about it?' people asked her.

'. . . is where the bomb struck.'

Swan Street was where Amy lived. She raced up the steps and out of the station, her heart thudding painfully as she ran back down the streets she'd recently walked along.

As Amy got closer to home, the smell of charred dust hung on the air. All around her firemen tried to contain the blazes caused by the incendiary bombs. At least one bomb, probably more, had landed in the rafters of a house, set that one on fire and then set several other houses either side of it alight as the fires spread.

'Mum! Dad!' she gasped with relief.

They were standing across the road from their house as the firemen put out the flames that had just started to take hold. Her mother had her face pressed against her father's shoulder and was crying as he held her to him. There was someone missing.

'Where's Grandpa?'

'He's missing,' her mother told her. 'And we don't know . . . don't know if he's . . .' She couldn't go on and hugged Amy to her.

Michael, Henry, Sky and Mr Ward screeched to a stop in the NARPAC ambulance.

'Amy, you OK?' Michael asked her as he jumped out.

Amy's voice cracked as she told him: 'My grandpa's missing.'

The ARP warden hurried over to tell Mr Ward which of the houses had pets in them. But before he could stop him Henry raced towards Amy's house and the open side gate that led to the back garden.

'Henry, come back!' Michael called as he ran after him. Michael knew he should have waited for the all-clear, but he couldn't let Henry get hurt.

'Stay back,' the fireman told Amy as she tried to follow too.

Henry stopped by a pile of rubble that had been the outside toilet, looked at Michael, wagged his tail and barked.

'What is it, Henry? Is there something there?'

Henry wagged his tail even faster and Michael started to lift the rubble away. Under it he found Amy's grandpa, covered in dust. Michael stretched out a hand and helped him to his feet. He'd got cuts and bruises, but otherwise didn't seem to be too badly injured.

'You're OK now,' Michael said as he pulled the old man's arm round his shoulders to support him.

'Misty,' the old man said, looking at Henry. 'Is that you, girl?'

Michael helped him out of the side gate and as soon as Mr and Mrs Dolan and Amy saw him they ran across the road to join him.

'Oh, Grandpa, you're alive!' Amy said, throwing her arms round the old man.

Mr Dolan took his coat off and put it round the old man's shoulders.

'Misty found me,' he said. 'She dug into the rubble and saved my life.'

'That's not Misty,' Amy told her grandpa. 'That's Henry.' Although sometimes Henry did remind her of Misty, and she felt a pang of sadness thinking of her and Jack's beloved dog.

She crouched down and stroked Henry, whose wildly wagging tail told her that he knew he'd done well.

'Good dog, Henry, good dog,' she said.

When they'd cleared up as best they could, Amy wrote to Jack to tell him about their house being bombed.

'Grandpa was there at the time, but the rest of us weren't, thank goodness. A rescue dog called Henry found him.'

She didn't mention that Grandpa had thought Misty had saved him because it would only make Jack sad that Misty still hadn't been found.

'*Henry's going to be part of the demonstration team for Lieutenant Colonel Richardson in a few weeks' time,*' she added to the letter. And hopefully, after that, Britain would very soon have its own national War Dog Training School once again.

Chapter 19

On the day of the demonstration Amy was at the Scout hut early to help set out the chairs and put the urn on for tea.

Ellie was very nervous when she arrived ten minutes later with Grace. 'I just want Lieutenant Colonel Richardson to understand how amazing these dogs are,' she said.

They'd all been practising for months, but she was still worried.

'It'll be fine,' Amy told her as Michael and Henry arrived.

'I hope so,' said Ellie. 'I don't want to let the dogs down.'

'You won't,' said Amy with a smile.

'Buster!' Michael said, a huge grin on his face as he and Henry went to say hello to the Jack Russell and his handler Alan. Buster stood on his hind legs and licked Michael's ear as he stroked him.

'Buster's my friend Robert's dog,' Michael told Amy. 'The one I told you about who went from

London to Devon and ended up as a search-and-rescue dog.'

'Never seen anyone as determined to do his job, whatever the danger, as this little guy,' Alan told Amy proudly. 'He's a proper star.'

Grace sniffed hello to an Airedale terrier called Beauty who was part of the People's Dispensary for Sick Animals rescue squad and had come with her owner Bill.

Amy was handing out mugs of tea when two Alsatians, Irma and Psyche, and their handler Margaret arrived. Amy had read about the lives the two dogs had saved with their rescue work in the national press and went to say hello.

Henry really took to a cross-breed dog called Rip and tried to play with him.

'Not now, Henry,' Michael told him.

'Rip's already rescued nearly a hundred people,' his handler said, 'and he's not done yet.'

Rip gave a play bark and Michael decided to keep the two dogs away from each other, in case they distracted one another during the demonstration.

Rip had been found when his own home had been bombed and from then on he'd taken to helping find others who'd been trapped in bombed-out buildings.

All the dogs from outside their local branch that had been invited had already found people buried under rubble during rescue missions. All of them had saved not just animal's lives, but people's lives too.

A hush fell over the room as word got round that Lieutenant Colonel Richardson had arrived. A few moments later the Scout hut door swung open and Mr Ward showed him in.

People looked round and their dogs looked up at them and round too, but didn't know what all the fuss was about.

Amy realized she'd forgotten to put a glass of water on the speaker's table and hurried to get one as the Lieutenant Colonel made his way to the front. Fortunately it took him a long time as he stopped to greet different dogs and their owners.

He had a soft spot for Alsatians.

'If we had more like you, we'd be victorious in no time,' he told Irma and Psyche, and Margaret smiled.

'We would indeed,' she said.

Amy held her breath as Ellie led the dogs in a demonstration, showing the Lieutenant Colonel what her search-and-rescue dogs could do. She could see he was impressed as the dogs used scent detection to find volunteers hidden in tunnels and under blankets and boxes. He laughed as Henry pulled off layers of cardboard box 'rubble' and then drew back a blanket to reveal Michael hidden underneath.

Henry's obvious excitement at finding his friend,

and his crazily wagging tail that looked like his whole body was joining in, reminded Amy of Misty again, especially when she was younger. But then lots of dogs reminded her of Misty – and made her think of how much she missed her still.

At the end of the demonstration everyone clapped and cheered. Lieutenant Colonel Richardson said he'd be reporting back on what he'd seen and hopefully there would be some good news about the War Dog Training School soon.

'That was fantastic,' Amy said to Ellie afterwards.

'Thanks,' she said.

As soon as the demonstration was over, Amy hurried off to join her parents and Grandpa at the station. She couldn't wait to tell them how well it had gone.

Daniel arrived at Wood Green Underground Station ten minutes before Amy did. The day he'd been knocked down had been the day that the lack of proper treatment for shell-shocked soldiers was widely reported in the press. Two psychiatrists, who'd been hired to deal with the sudden increase in shell shock after Dunkirk, had resigned in protest and the Ministry for Health had organized a nationwide network of mind hospitals.

Daniel had been treated for his physical injuries at North Middlesex and then transferred to a mind hospital. There he'd been given daily counselling and medication to help with the symptoms. Good food and a proper bed to sleep in had also helped. Day by day he began to return to himself, not quite able to look his psychiatrist in the eye yet. But his psychiatrist had been pleased with his progress.

'A few more months here and you should be much better. I can see you've been through a tough time,' he'd said.

But Daniel didn't want to stay at the hospital for a few more months. He was worried about Howl and how frightened and confused the puppy must have been when he was taken away in the ambulance.

What had happened to Howl afterwards? Had he gone back to the Underground or had he been picked up by one of the dog wardens? At least he'd got his mum's collar on. Daniel was glad about that. They couldn't put the pup down when he was wearing one of those. But still he worried about Howl and early one morning, as the sun was coming up, he left the hospital to find him.

As he entered the station, Daniel looked a lot different to the man that had been lying injured in the road. He was fatter, for one thing. Plus, the nurses had found him some new clothes in the charity box, and he'd had his hair cut and was bathed and shaved. But, kind as they'd been there, he needed to see if the puppy who'd meant so much to him was OK and still living in the Underground.

He longed to see Soldier again, but part of him also hoped that the puppy wasn't there any more. That someone had taken pity on the dog and taken it home to live with them.

In Daniel's old room at the station Howl gnawed on the ham bone he'd found in one of the pig bins, as the first of the Underground's night visitors arrived.

Howl smelt the familiar smell almost as soon as Daniel stepped into the station. It made his heart race with excitement.

'Soldier,' Daniel said softly, and Howl looked up and then he was up and racing to him as fast as his legs would go. He jumped into Daniel's arms, almost toppling a laughing Daniel over, and then Howl couldn't stop licking him because he was so pleased to see his friend.

And Daniel couldn't stop laughing either; he'd missed the puppy so badly. He laughed so hard that tears ran down his face and Howl licked them up.

'Good dog,' said Daniel. 'Good dog, Soldier.'

Sky raced to the front door as soon as she heard the car rattle to a stop. Her paw was bandaged where she'd cut it on some glass during her last search-and-rescue mission with Mr Ward, but it didn't stop her. Heggerty, although slower, was not far behind.

'Let me get to the door then,' Mrs Ward said, pushing her way past them.

She was a little surprised to find her husband and son had brought Lieutenant Colonel Richardson home with them. But very little fazed her these days – the war had seen to that.

'Come in, come in,' she said as Henry breezed past her, his tail wagging.

Mrs Ward made sandwiches and laid them out on the top of the two-tier Morrison shelter that they now used as a table.

'Bee in a bonnet, bee in a bonnet,' the parrot said in greeting as soon as the Lieutenant Colonel walked into the room.

'You're honoured,' Mr Ward told him. 'Haven't heard that one before.'

'I made these for Henry while you were all out,' Mrs Ward said, holding up four dog-sized boots. 'They'll protect his paws from the glass and rubble when he's on his rescue missions. We don't want any more accidents like Sky's if we can help it.'

'What did you make them from?' Mr Ward asked suspiciously. The tartan material looked very familiar. 'Are those my slippers?'

'They'll be nice and flexible but strong at the same time,' Mrs Ward said. 'And I didn't just chop up your slippers. I chopped up mine to make some for Sky too.'

Michael tried one on Henry.

'What do you think?'

Henry wagged his tail.

'I think they're an excellent idea,' Lieutenant Colonel Richardson said.

'Won't you have a sandwich?' Mrs Ward said. 'The eggs are from our chickens.'

Lieutenant Colonel Richardson had just helped himself when the parrot started squawking.

'Bombs away! Bombs away!' It flew off its perch and into the top part of the Morrison shelter.

'Quick, get all the animals in with him,' Mr Ward said.

'Because a parrot's squawking bombs away?' Lieutenant Colonel Richardson said, bewildered.

'He's our early-warning system,' said Mrs Ward.

'Never been wrong yet,' Michael told him, picking up the kitten. And right on cue they heard Wailing Winnie, a nickname they'd all come to use for the air-raid siren's shrill cry.

'Everybody in,' said Mr Ward. 'It'll be a bit of a squeeze, but we'll manage.'

'Mummy's *po-ppet*, Mummy's *po-ppet*,' the parrot squawked in a panic.

''S all right,' Mr Ward told him. 'Keep your hair on.'

'Keep your hair on, keep your hair on,' the parrot repeated over and over.

Michael held the kitten close as they listened to the whistle of incendiary bombs followed by the boom as the bombs struck. He counted three, no four, bombs close by.

The house shook and everything that could fall did fall: the plaster came down from the ceiling and the wall cracked in two. Debris landed in a clatter on top of the Morrison shelter. It was noisy and frightening, but inside the shelter they were safe.

Chapter 20

The bomb hit with such force that it knocked Daniel and Howl to the ground. Daniel lay very still and Howl crawled over to him, put his head on his friend's chest and whined. Daniel didn't stir.

On the platform people were thrown on to the railway tracks. The lights immediately went out. For a second or two there was a shocked silence, swiftly followed by screaming and mayhem as people panicked.

Mrs Dolan took Amy's and her father's hand. Mr Dolan switched on the torch he always kept with him for emergencies and soon others did the same. It was hard to tell who'd been injured and how badly they'd been hurt in the blast because it was so dark. People bumped into each other, stumbled and fell. Those nearest the stairs headed towards them, people behind them followed them upwards and soon almost everyone was trying to go up. They shoved each other in their panic to get up the stairs and out.

'Out of my way.'

'Who you shoving?'

'Why aren't we moving?'

'Get on up there.'

But the people at the front, who'd gone up the stairs already, soon found the exit was blocked.

'Help, let us out,' they shouted from behind the rubble. There was no reply.

Close by, Daniel opened his eyes at last and Howl licked his face. But Daniel barely even felt the lick. All the terror and trauma of being at Dunkirk came crashing down on him; his heart raced and he felt like he couldn't breathe as his body shook uncontrollably as panic overcame him.

Howl's own fear of the bomb was surpassed by his fear for his friend. He whined and paced back and forth, unsure what to do, as Daniel staggered to his feet and made agonizing sounds as he gasped for breath.

'Go, Soldier, leave me,' Daniel groaned.

Howl whined again and put his paw out as Daniel sank to his knees. The dog wagged his tail, still unsure, but then he ran for the platform as Daniel collapsed back onto the ground.

The people at the end of the queue to get up the stairs didn't at first realize what the hold-up was and were angry it wasn't moving forward. Then word came back down the platform, in a trickle at first, that there was a problem getting out via the steps. The trickle turned into a torrent as the panic of being trapped in the Underground, with more bombs likely to strike, grew.

'What's going to happen to us?'

'How are we going to get out?'

'I don't want to die down here.'

The panic increased and rose until it was almost unstoppable. Mr Dolan knew that if it were allowed to continue none of them would get out alive.

'Stay calm,' he shouted to those around him. 'Keep calm!'

But most people were too frightened to listen.

As her eyes grew accustomed to the darkness, Amy saw the dog she'd shared sandwiches with a few weeks ago. She hadn't seen it since the bomb went off in Swan Street and had presumed it had left the station.

'What's Misty doing here?' Amy's grandfather asked her, noticing Howl too.

'It's not Misty, Grandpa,' Amy told him, although the dog did look very similar to Misty in the dark. 'Hello,' she said to the dog as she stretched her hand out to him. She didn't want him to be frightened.

But Howl didn't let her touch him; as Amy stepped forward, he backed away a few paces, then stopped and whined. Amy took another two steps towards him and the same thing happened.

'I think he wants us to follow him,' she said to her family.

Howl kept checking behind him to make sure Amy was following him as he led her and her mother and father and Grandpa through the disused tunnel to Daniel's room.

There was more light there and Amy stopped, unsure what to do when she saw Daniel. He couldn't stop shaking and had his hands to his throat as he made horrible wheezing sounds. But then Amy's grandpa stepped forward.

'I've seen this before in the Great War,' he said. 'It's shock.' Daniel was having a panic attack and he needed to slow down his breathing. If he'd had a paper bag, Amy's grandpa would have given Daniel that to breathe into.

'Here, son, put this over your mouth and breathe into it,' he said as he pulled his handkerchief from his pocket and gave it to Daniel. 'Slow breaths now. That's it . . . Keep them slow.'

Daniel did as he was told and gradually, as they all watched nervously, his breathing settled.

'Th-thank you,' he said.

Amy's grandpa nodded.

'What are we going to do now?' Amy asked. To her surprise, it was Daniel who spoke next.

'Out, Soldier, out,' he said to Howl. It was the word Daniel used when they were going to the park.

'If anyone can find a way out of this station, he can,' Daniel explained.

There are many parts of Underground stations that most people never get to see: disused pipes and tunnels, platforms that are shut off, even stairways that are no longer used.

Howl had lived in Wood Green Underground his whole life and he knew every inch of it. Although some parts – the 'people' parts – he rarely went into unless there was no one about.

The station being plunged into darkness didn't matter to Howl. He could find his way just as easily whether it was light or dark. First he headed back out to the platform.

Mr Dolan motioned to the family who had been sitting next to them and explained that the skinny dog might be able to find a way out. Quickly word spread down the platform. Then the family beside that family followed too and soon Howl was leading all the people along the disused rail track and through the secret passages and tunnels of the station.

At last, the all-clear siren went off. Michael and the others crawled out of the Morrison shelter and ran to the front door. The bombs had seemed so close, closer and more violent than ever before.

'I'll stay behind and see to the animals,' Mrs

Ward said. There was dust and plaster everywhere, but judging from the loud racket the animals were making she didn't think any of them were too badly hurt.

'Hush now,' she said. 'Hush now, you're all right.'

'Hush now, hush now,' the parrot repeated after her.

Sky ran to the front door after the rest of them.

'No, Sky, not you. You can't go,' Mrs Ward told her. Sky whined, but Mrs Ward shook her head. 'Not today.' She couldn't risk Sky's paw getting even more injured than it already was.

Lieutenant Colonel Richardson was already at the door. Michael took Henry with them.

'Be careful,' Mrs Ward said as she held on to Sky's collar.

'We will.'

At first, the damage didn't seem too bad, but when they turned the corner of the road that led to the station they could only stare in horror. Wood Green wasn't even recognizable as a station any more. It looked like it had imploded on itself. The curved front of the station was crushed and flattened.

The first of the fire engines raced past them, bells clattering. An ambulance followed close behind. And behind that came a Women's Voluntary Service van with blankets and food.

When they reached the station, coughing because

of all the smoke, Michael stopped and stared, aghast.

'Do you think . . . anyone's . . .' He couldn't say it aloud. He knew that Amy and her family often sheltered in the Underground station. Lieutenant Colonel Richardson squeezed his shoulder.

But could anyone have survived the blast? The bomb had caused catastrophic damage. The station looked like a tower of building bricks that had been toppled over and now lay in a haphazard and confused mess, spilling its contents across the road.

Chapter 21

Howl stopped and everyone behind him stopped too. The exit via the pig bins, which should have been ahead of them, was totally blocked by debris. But Howl had noticed a strange sound too, one that he'd never heard before. By the time other people heard the creak there wasn't time to get away.

With a mighty crash a steel casing over the back staircase gave way, sending soot, wet earth, sludge and other debris down in front of them, blocking the path ahead. Amy's family were at the front and so were Daniel and Howl, and they bore the brunt. Daniel suddenly realized that he could no longer see Howl.

'Soldier,' he cried. 'Soldier.'

The soot and wet earth was up to a man's knees. More than enough to suffocate a dog if it came tumbling down on him.

'Soldier,' Daniel bellowed, and this time it was more the desperate cry of an animal than a man.

Over and over he dug his hands deep into the wet earth and Amy, her grandpa and mum and dad did too.

But then Daniel heard a small sound coming from one of the bins. In an instant he had waded through the mud to reach his dog.

'Good Soldier, at ease, Soldier,' he said as he pulled a smelly, mud- and soot-covered Howl from the top of an overflowing pig bin that had probably saved his life.

Howl licked the mud on his friend's face and Daniel laughed as he hugged Howl's muddy, wet but still warm body to him.

'Out, Soldier,' Daniel said again. 'Out.' He knew they had no time to lose. The station was clearly unstable and could collapse around them at any moment.

Howl sent out little mud sprays as he wagged his mud-encased tail. He wanted to go out, but their exit was blocked by the sludge. They'd have to go back the way they'd come. But that way was blocked by the people crowding in from the tunnel behind them.

All of these people were frightened near to panic, and many were not even quite sure what had happened because of the darkness and being further away.

Beside the ledge, up on the wall where Sheba used to watch from, there was a hole with a twisted metal grating in front of it. Howl barked up at it.

Mr Dolan pulled the grating away and looked into the hole. It was filled with rubble, but he could just make out a small gleam of daylight at the end of it.

Howl whined and Mr Dolan stepped back as Daniel lifted the dog into the tunnel hole. Howl crawled on his belly through the dust and debris to the light. He could hear voices ahead of him and then he heard a bark he recognized and crawled faster.

Amy was helped into the hole and crawled behind Howl, but there wasn't enough space for her to get as far along as the dog had been able to. She was trapped in a narrow space with debris all around her and dust choking her.

Outside the tunnel that Howl and Amy had gone down there was another ominous creaking sound. But there was nothing anyone could do and nowhere for them to run.

'This way!'

Michael ran down Lordship Lane and up Berners Lane and into Hardy Passage to reach the back of the station. Here the bomb damage, although still terrible, wasn't quite so bad as at the front. Henry suddenly raced towards one particular spot of rubble and started pawing at it and whining. Then he began to dig at the rubble so frantically that his paws got cut on the sharp brick edges that had come falling down as the station walls collapsed.

'No, Henry!' Michael said when he saw the blood coming from Henry's cut pads. 'No more digging.' He didn't want Henry's paws getting infected.

Just at that moment they heard it: a long drawn-out mournful howl coming from under the ground.

All at once they started lifting away the rubble where Henry had dug. Henry whined and tried to do what Michael said, waiting for the rubble to be cleared. But then the howl came again and Henry couldn't wait any longer. He tore and scratched at the rubble, then looked up at Michael and wagged his tail.

Everyone now helped to remove the debris. Mr Ward and Lieutenant Colonel Richardson made them form a line and they passed it along to each other, moving it away from the damaged site so as not to cause a cave-in. As more rubble was removed, they heard a girl's voice shout.

'We're down here!'

'Amy?' Michael shouted back.

'Yes.'

'Don't worry, we're going to get you out.' But Michael knew they were all in great danger of the station collapsing from under them, trapping Amy and the other people inside, or worse, crushing them.

The rubble removal quickened and a few minutes later Henry started running backwards and forwards excitedly. Then he began barking and when they looked they could see why – a soot- and mud-covered nose was poking out. And soon it wasn't just a nose, it was Howl. At last, helped by the slipperiness of the mud that coated and soaked his fur, he was able to wriggle himself out.

Howl was not a pretty sight and he definitely didn't smell sweet either, but Henry was overjoyed to see him. The brothers' tails wagged and they sniffed and licked each other's faces.

Amy pushed against the rubble, sending stones and cement flying as she forced her way after Howl. The dust stung her eyes so much she could barely see as tears ran down her face. The rough masonry tore into her skin, but she pushed on and then suddenly she wasn't pushing; she wasn't feeling anything but air.

'I'm here, I'm here,' she cried. She felt a hand grab hers.

'You're all right, you're going to be all right,' Michael said.

They removed more rubble from the ventilation access tunnel and Amy was able to crawl out.

Then the firemen and the civilian defence came with their equipment and made the NARPAC group move out of the way as they dug downwards and one by one more people, an endless line of people, crawled out of the rubble and into the fresh air.

Amy threw her arms round Michael when she saw him and he hugged her back, not caring that she was covered in smelly mud. He was just so glad his friend was alive.

'If it wasn't for that dog!' Amy said. She could barely think straight, but she still wanted to tell Michael what had happened. As she spoke, mud slipped into her mouth and she wiped it away. 'We followed him . . .'

'That's twice Misty's saved me,' said Amy's grandfather as he was helped out of the tunnel to the surface by Michael from in front and Daniel from behind.

The old man blinked as he saw Henry and Howl playing together among the rubble. 'Two Mistys?' he said.

'Misty isn't here, Grandpa,' Amy told him. Neither of the two dogs had Misty's distinctive cream-coloured fur. Henry's was tan and white and the other dog – well, it was quite hard to know exactly what he looked like under all that mud and soot. The dogs' body shapes and ears did look similar, but the second dog was slighter than Henry was.

'Look at those two,' Michael grinned as he watched Henry and Howl playing together. 'You'd think they'd known each other for years rather than just met.'

'That's dogs for you,' said Lieutenant Colonel Richardson. It was one of the many reasons he liked working with them so much. 'None of the fuss and suspicions of people, just a quick sniff and they're friends for life.'

Daniel had been quiet until that moment, but he wanted Amy and Michael to know the truth.

'They're brothers,' he said from behind them. 'Born in the Underground at the start of the Blitz.'

'But what was Misty doing down in the Underground?' Amy's grandfather said loudly as a WVS lady handed him a cup of sweet tea.

'It isn't Misty, Grandpa,' Amy said. 'They're boys for a start!'

Daniel overheard her. 'Their mother was called Misty,' he said. 'Soldier's got her collar on round his neck. Bark and Howl – that's what I liked to call them when they were puppies. But then Bark disappeared one day.'

'I found him and took him home,' said Michael. 'But we call him Henry now.'

Amy went over to Howl, who was now sitting with Henry and watching the proceedings. It was hard to even tell that he was wearing a collar or had an ID disc round his neck because of all the mud.

'Hello, Howl,' she said, crouching down. Amy reached out to look at the name tag on his collar, then sat back on her heels in shock. 'Misty,' she murmured.

Amy looked over at Daniel. 'She ran away on the first night of the Blitz. I looked and looked for her. But I never thought to look inside the Underground.'

'I put her collar on Howl,' Daniel told her. 'I thought it'd keep him safe – being properly registered and all.'

'But what about Misty?' Amy asked him.

Daniel shook his head and looked down at his muddy borrowed shoes. 'She was a good mother to her pups. Without her love and care in their first few months they'd have had no chance of being here now. They meant everything to her.'

He remembered his first meeting with her at the pig bins and how brave she was, always trying to protect her pups. He swallowed hard.

'I wish I could have done more for her. But I didn't realize how sick she was until I found her body.'

'Poor Misty,' Amy said as tears slipped down her face. 'All alone.'

'She had a friend,' said Daniel. 'A brave friend who looked out for her and the pups.' And he told Amy about the one-eared cat that he'd buried next to Misty.

Amy's eyes glittered with tears. 'She'd have been really proud of what heroes her pups have become,' she said as she stroked Howl.

'Proper little soldiers,' agreed Daniel.

Henry came over to Michael for strokes too, not wanting to be forgotten. Amy cuddled Howl to her and he stretched up his neck for his chin to be stroked, just like Misty used to do.

She smiled at Daniel, but he was looking at Howl rather than her and didn't notice. She was glad he'd been able to tell her the story of Misty and her pups. Then she frowned, wondering how Daniel could know all of this, and realized he must have been living in the Underground too. She looked at him again; he was still very pale and had started shaking.

Just then the WVS ladies came over with tea and buns. One of them put a blanket round Daniel's shoulders and gave him a cup of sweet tea. He hadn't long recovered from his accident and the day's events had taken it out of him.

'Thank you.'

He watched as Howl played with his brother and was fussed over by everyone. The Dolans would give the pup a good home and regular meals. Howl would have a better life with them than living with a homeless man.

He'd come back today because he couldn't bear to think of Howl all alone in the Underground. But really he had so little to offer him it would be better, kinder, to let him go with someone else.

It didn't matter that it would break his heart to

lose him. All that mattered was what was best for Howl. Daniel thought it would be best to quietly slip away before they asked him any more questions.

But as soon as Daniel started to walk away Howl looked over at him and howled. Amy hurried over to stop him from leaving.

Lieutenant Colonel Richardson had been listening and frowned as he watched her. He'd seen men like Daniel before. Men who'd been traumatized by the war, who'd seen such horror they didn't feel able to go home again. Men who felt guilt that they'd been saved while other good men had died. Men who didn't feel they deserved to be happy or have a normal life any more.

And the dog had too much potential to let him go now. And there was hope, even for men like Daniel. He could see what a special bond man and dog had.

'That dog's needed for the war effort,' he said. 'And he'll need you to be his handler, soldier, if we're to get the best from him.'

'Me?' said Daniel. 'But I . . . How did you know I was a soldier?'

'Once he's fully trained, he'll be able to help even more people: both civilians like he did today and also soldiers on the battlefield,' Lieutenant Colonel Richardson continued, as if Daniel hadn't spoken.

Daniel hadn't been able to save his fellow soldiers

at Dunkirk or the men who'd drowned when their boat was hit just outside Dover, but maybe together he and Howl could help to save someone else.

He buried his face in Howl's fur and whispered, 'I won't let you down, Soldier.'

'So is the War Dog Training School going to go ahead then?' Amy asked Lieutenant Colonel Richardson.

'Most definitely!' he said. 'I'd say it's imperative for this country's victory.'

Amy and Michael grinned at each other. Ellie was going to be over the moon when she heard.

'It'd be a good idea, in the mean time, to take your dog along to Ellie's training classes,' Mr Ward said to Daniel.

'Henry loves going there and I bet your dog will too,' Michael told Daniel.

'You and your dog are welcome to stay with us until you go off to the War Dog Training School,' Mr Dolan said.

'Misty should be in her own home,' Amy's grandfather agreed.

And this time Amy didn't contradict him. Tonight she'd write and let Jack know that, in one way, Misty had been found.

'It'd be nice to have one of Misty's puppies staying at our house,' she said.

'We'd be honoured to have you both,' Mr Dolan told Daniel.

'Thank you.' Daniel smiled. He was ready to take his first step into his new life.

Howl gave Daniel's ear a lick and then ran back to his brother. He play-bowed to him and Henry accepted the invitation with a dip of his own in return.

Daniel watched with Amy and Michael as Henry and Howl played among the rubble and devastation of the Blitz, just as they'd once played together underground. Together again at last.

Afterword

When I sat down to write *The Victory Dogs*, my aim was to create a story that was as believable and realistic as possible. But it is fiction rather than non-fiction, and not true. A bomb didn't really strike Wood Green Underground station in World War II, although the station next to it on the Piccadilly Line, Bounds Green, was badly damaged and there's a memorial plaque to the nineteen people who lost their lives there.

A man named Lieutenant Colonel Richardson did really set up the War Dog School in World War I and was instrumental in it eventually being reformed in World War II. The visiting dogs at Ellie's demonstration, apart from Buster, who was in *The Great Escape*, were all Dickin Medal winners. Beauty, Irma, Psyche and Rip really did save countless lives.

The Dickin Medal is awarded to animals for 'acts of conspicuous gallantry and devotion to duty in wartime'. The medal was instituted in 1943 and named after the PDSA founder, Mrs Maria Dickin CBE.

During World War II, a total of fifty-four Dickin Medals were awarded, of which thirty-two went to pigeons, eighteen to dogs, three to horses and one to a cat.

Animals never choose to go to war but they often show us how to be true heroes.

Acknowledgements

Huge thanks are due to the many people that graciously gave of their time and shared their knowledge with me during the researching of this book. Special thanks go to Bill Davies for his help with my many train tunnel questions and to his long-time train-travelling companion Labrador Rescue dog and total star, Harvey, for always making me smile. Thanks as well to Christopher and Shirley Butcher for their stories of North London in the Blitz and to their cat, Sooty, who sat on my lap and watched me type (awkwardly) on my laptop. And special thanks to my mum and dad, Jim and Sylvia, who are always so supportive, had once played as children in Lordship Recreation Ground and, most helpfully of all, had had a very intelligent, talking bird.

Congratulations go to Nicole Mulholland who won *The Great Escape*'s Young Times/Puffin My Pet My Hero competition. Her prize was to name a character in my next book – which is this one.

She chose her dog Sky's name. Sky helped the family's cat, BJ, by acting as a guide dog when BJ went blind.

Visits to the Imperial War Museum in London and Duxford were enlightening and entertaining, and my trip to the London Transport Museum resulted in me changing my station clerk from a man to a woman. Thanks also to the staff at the London Transport Museum for their generous help with my research.

On the writing side I would like to thank my agent Clare Pearson, of Eddison Pearson, and my editors at Puffin, Shannon Cullen and Anthea Townsend, whose endless encouragement helped this book to reach its full potential; also thanks to Samantha Mackintosh and Jane Tait for their meticulous copy-editing – all of whom I hope I'm lucky enough to work with on future books.

Part of this book was written in a spare consulting room at Davies Veterinary Specialist Hospital where my dog Traffy was being treated. I believe her consultant and surgeon, Aidan McAlinden, saved her life and I will always be grateful. Thankfully, Traffy is once again able to enjoy playing with our other dog, and her best friend, Bella. She's now eating all her food with relish and back to taking up far more than her fair share of the bed.

Finally, and as always, thanks to my wonderful husband, who spent hours helping with my research for this book and whose love and enthusiasm make writing a joy.

Turn the page for an extract from

The Great Escape

by Megan Rix

AVAILABLE NOW

Chapter 1

On a steamy hot Saturday morning in the summer of 1939, a Jack Russell with a patch of tan fur over his left eye and a black spot over his right was digging as though his life depended upon it.

His little white forepaws attacked the soft soil, sending chrysanthemums, stocks and freesias to their deaths. He'd soon dug so deep that the hole was bigger than he was, and all that could be seen were sprays of flying soil and his fiercely wagging tail.

'Look at Buster go,' twelve-year-old Robert Edwards said, leaning on his spade. 'He could win a medal for his digging.'

Robert's best friend, Michael, laughed. 'Bark when you reach Australia!' he told Buster's rear end. He tipped the soil from his shovel on to the fast-growing mound beside them.

Buster's tail wagged as he emerged from the hole triumphant, his muddy treasure gripped firmly in his mouth.

'Oh no, better get that off him!' Robert said, when he realized what Buster had.

'What is it?' Michael asked.

'One of Dad's old slippers – he's been looking for them everywhere.'

'But how did it get down there?'

Buster cocked his head to one side, his right ear up and his left ear down.

'*Someone* must have buried it there. Buster – give!'

But Buster had no intention of giving up his treasure. As Robert moved closer to him Buster danced backwards.

'Buster – Buster – give it to me!'

Robert and Michael raced around the garden after Buster, trying to get the muddy, chewed slipper from him. Buster thought this was a wonderful new game of chase, and almost lost the slipper by barking with excitement as he dodged this way and that.

The game got even better when Robert's nine-year-old sister Lucy, and Rose the collie, came out of the house and started to chase him too.

'Buster, come back . . .'

Rose tried to circle him and cut him off. Until recently she'd been a sheepdog and she was much quicker than Buster, but he managed to evade her by jumping over the ginger-and-white cat, Tiger, who wasn't pleased to be used as a fence and hissed at Buster to tell him so.

Buster was having such a good time. First digging

up the flower bed, now playing chase. It was the perfect day – until Lucy dived on top of him and he was trapped.

'Got you!'

Robert took Dad's old slipper from Buster. 'Sorry, but you can't play with that.'

Buster jumped up at the slipper, trying to get it back. It was his – he'd buried it and he'd dug it up. Robert held the slipper above his head so Buster couldn't get it, although for such a small dog, he could jump pretty high.

Buster went back to his hole and started digging to see if he could find something else interesting. Freshly dug soil was soon flying into the air once again.

'No slacking, you two!' Robert's father, Mr Edwards, told the boys as he came out of the back door. Robert quickly hid the slipper behind him; he didn't want Buster to get into trouble. Michael took it from him, unseen.

Lucy ran back into the kitchen, with Rose close behind her.

'You two should be following Buster's example,' Mr Edwards said to the boys.

At the sound of his name Buster stopped digging for a moment and emerged from his hole. His face was covered in earth and it was clear that he was in his element. Usually he'd have been in huge trouble for digging in the garden, but not today. When

Mr Edwards wasn't looking, Michael dropped the slipper into the small ornamental fishpond near to where Tiger was lying. Tiger rubbed his head against Michael's hand, the bell on his collar tinkling softly, and Michael obligingly stroked him behind his ginger ears before getting back to work.

Tiger had been out on an early-morning prowl of the neighbourhood when the government truck had arrived and the men from it had rung the doorbell of every house along the North London terraced street. Each homeowner had been given six curved sheets of metal, two steel plates and some bolts for fixing it all together.

'There you go.'

'Shouldn't take you more than a few hours.'

'Got hundreds more of these to deliver.'

Four of the workmen helped those who couldn't manage to put up their own Anderson Shelters, but everyone else was expected to dig a large hole in their back garden, deep enough so that only two feet of the six-foot-high bomb shelter could be seen above the ground.

Buster, Robert and Michael had set to work as soon as they'd been given theirs, with Mr Edwards supervising.

'Is the hole big enough yet, Dad?' Robert asked his father. They'd been digging for ages.

Mr Edwards peered at the government instruction leaflet and shook his head. 'It needs to be four foot deep in the soil. And we'll need to dig steps down to the door.'

Tiger surveyed the goings-on through half-closed eyes from his favourite sunspot on the patio. He was content to watch as Buster wore himself out and got covered in mud. It was much too hot a day to do anything as energetic as digging.

In the kitchen, Rose was getting in the way as usual.

'Let me past, Rose,' said Lucy and Robert's mother, Mrs Edwards, turning away from the window.

Rose took a step or two backwards, but she was still in the way. The Edwardses' kitchen was small, but they'd managed to cram a wooden dresser as well as two wooden shelves and a cupboard into it. It didn't have a refrigerator.

'What were you all doing out there?' Mrs Edwards asked Lucy.

Lucy thought it best not to mention that Buster had dug up Dad's old slipper. It was from Dad's favourite pair and Mum had turned the house upside-down searching for it.

'Just playing,' she said.

Lucy began squeezing six lemon halves into a brown earthenware jug while her mother made sugar syrup by adding a cup of water and a cup of sugar to a saucepan and bringing it to the boil on the coal gas stove. Wearing a full-length apron over her button-down dress, Mrs Edwards stirred continuously so as not to scorch the syrup or the pan.

The letterbox rattled and Lucy went to see what it was. Another government leaflet lay on the mat. They seemed to be getting them almost every day now. This one had 'Sand to the Rescue' written in big letters and gave instructions on how to place sandbags so that they shielded the windows, and how to dispose of incendiary bombs using a sand-bucket and scoop.

Lucy put the leaflet on the dresser with the others and went to check on her cakes. She didn't want them to burn, especially not with Michael visiting.

Two hours later Mr Edwards declared, 'That should be enough.'

Robert and Michael stopped digging and admired their work. Buster, however, wasn't ready to stop yet. He wanted them to dig a second, even bigger hole, and he knew exactly where that hole should be. His little paws got busy digging in the new place.

'No, Buster, no more!' Robert said firmly.

Buster stopped and sat down. He watched as Robert, Michael and Mr Edwards assembled the Anderson Shelter from the six corrugated iron sheets and end plates, which they bolted together at the top.

'Right, that's it, easy does it,' Mr Edwards told the boys. The Anderson Shelter was up and in place.

For the first time Tiger became interested. The

shelter looked like a new choice sunspot – especially when the sun glinted on its corrugated iron top. He uncurled himself and sauntered over to it.

'Hello, Tiger. Come to have a look?' Michael asked him. Tiger ignored the question, jumped on to the top of the shelter and curled up on the roof.

Robert and Michael laughed. 'He must be the laziest cat in the world,' Robert said. 'All he does is eat and sleep and then sleep again.'

Tiger's sunbathing was cut short.

'You can't sleep there, Tiger,' Mr Edwards said. 'And we can't have the roof glinting in the sunshine like that. Go on – scat, cat.'

Tiger ran a few feet away and then stopped and watched as Mr Edwards and the boys now shovelled the freshly dug soil pile they'd made back on top of the roof of the bomb shelter, with Buster trying to help by digging at the pile – which wasn't really any help at all.

Mr Edwards wiped his brow as he stopped to look at the instruction leaflet again. 'It says it needs to be covered with at least fifteen inches of soil above the roof,' he told Robert and Michael.

The three of them kept on shovelling until the shelter was completely hidden by the newly dug soil.

Lucy and Mrs Edwards came out, carrying freshly made lemonade and fairy cakes.

'Good, we've earned this,' Robert said when he saw them.

'Those look very appetizing, Lucy love,' Mr Edwards said when Lucy held out the plate of cakes.

'Do you like it?' Lucy asked Michael, as he bit into his cake. Her eyes were shining.

'Delicious,' Michael smiled, and took another bite.

Buster was desperate to taste one of Lucy's cakes too. He looked at her meaningfully, mouth open, tail wagging winningly. When that didn't work he tried sitting down and lifting his paws in the air in a begging position.

Lucy furtively nudged one of the cakes off the plate on to the ground.

'Oops!'

Buster was on it and the cake was gone in one giant gulp. He looked up hopefully for more.

Mr Edwards took a long swig of his lemonade and put his beaker back on the tray. 'So, what do you think?' he asked his wife.

Mrs Edwards's flower garden was ruined. 'It's going to make it very awkward to hang out the weekly washing.'

'In a few weeks' time even I'd have trouble spotting it from the air,' Mr Edwards said. He was a reconnaissance pilot and was used to navigating from landmarks on the ground. 'It'll be covered in weeds and grass and I bet we could even grow flowers or tomato plants on it if we wanted to.'

Lucy grinned. 'But you'd still know we were nearby and wave to us from your plane, wouldn't you, Dad?'

'I would,' smiled Mr Edwards. 'With Alexandra Palace just round the corner, our street is hard to miss. But Jerry flying over with his bombs won't have a clue the Anderson Shelter's down here with you hidden inside it – and that's the main thing.'

Lucy shivered. 'Will there really be another war, Dad?' It was a question everyone was asking.

'I hope not. I really do,' Mr Edwards said, putting his arm round his wife. 'They called the last one the Great War and told us it was the war to end all wars. But now that looks doubtful.'

Michael helped himself to another of Lucy's cakes and smiled at her.

Lucy was beaming as she went back inside, with Rose following her.

As Lucy filled Buster's bowl with fresh water and took it back outside, Rose padded behind her like a shadow. She chose different people, and occasionally Buster or Tiger, to follow on different days. But she chose Lucy most of all. She'd tried to herd Buster and Tiger once or twice, as she used to do with the sheep, but so far this hadn't been very successful, due to Buster and Tiger's lack of cooperation.

'Here, Buster, you must be thirsty too after all that digging,' Lucy said, putting his water bowl down on the patio close to Tiger, who stretched out his legs and flexed his sharp claws. Lucy stroked him and Tiger purred.

Buster lapped at the water with his little pink tongue.

'Buster deserves a bone for all that digging,' Robert said. 'Or at least a biscuit or two.'

Buster looked up at him and wagged his tail.

'Go on then,' Mrs Edwards said.

Robert went inside and came back with Buster's tin of dog biscuits. Buster wagged his tail even more enthusiastically at the sight of the tin, and wolfed down the biscuit Robert gave him. Bones or biscuits – food was food.

'Here, Rose, want a biscuit?' Robert asked her.

Rose accepted one and then went to lie down beside the bench on which Lucy was sitting. She preferred it when everyone was together in the same place; only then could she really settle.

Just a few months ago Rose had been living in Devon and working as a sheepdog. But things had changed when the elderly farmer didn't come out one morning, or the next. Rose waited for the farmer at the back door from dawn to dusk and then went back to the barn where she slept. But the farmer never came.

Some days the farmer's wife brought a plate of food for her. Some days she forgot and Rose went to sleep hungry.

Then the farmer's daughter, Mrs Edwards, came to the farm, dressed in black, and the next day she took Rose back to London with her on the train. Rose never saw the farmer again.

Rose whined and Lucy bent and stroked her head.

'Feeling sad?' she asked her.

Sometimes Rose had a faraway look in her eyes that made Lucy wonder just what Rose was thinking. Did she miss Devon? It must be strange for Rose only having a small garden to run about in when she was used to herding sheep with her grandfather on the moor.

'Do you miss Grandad?'

Rose licked Lucy's hand.

'I miss him too,' Lucy said.

When they all went back indoors, Tiger stayed in the garden. He took a step closer to the Anderson Shelter and then another step and another. Tiger was a very curious sort of cat, and being shooed away had only made him more curious. He ran down the earth steps and peered into the new construction.

Inside it was dark, but felt cool and slightly damp after the heat of the sun.

'Tiger!' Lucy called, coming back out. 'Tiger, where are you?'

Lucy came down the garden and found him.

'There you are. Why didn't you come when I called you?' She picked Tiger up like a baby, with his paws waving in the air, and carried him out of the shelter and back up to the house. It wasn't the most comfortable or dignified way of travelling, but Tiger put up with it because it was Lucy. Ever since Tiger had arrived at the Edwardses' house as a tiny mewling kitten, he and Lucy had had a special bond.

They stopped at the living room where Robert was showing Michael Buster's latest trick.

'Slippers, Buster,' Robert said.

Buster raced to the shoe rack by the front door, found Robert's blue leather slippers and raced back with one of them in his mouth. He dropped the slipper beside Robert.

Robert put his foot in it and said, 'Slippers,' again. Buster raced off and came back with the other one.

Robert gave him a dog biscuit.

Michael grinned. 'He's so smart.'

'He can identify Dad and Mum and Lucy's slippers too,' Robert told Michael. He'd decided not to risk Dad's new slippers with Buster today. 'You're one clever dog, aren't you, Buster?'

Buster wagged his tail like mad and then raced round and round, chasing it.

'Tiger and Rose can do tricks too,' Lucy said, putting Tiger down in an armchair. 'And Rose doesn't need to be bribed with food to do them. Look – down, Rose.'

Rose obediently lay down.

Lucy moved across the room and Rose started to stand up to follow her.

'Stay, Rose.'

Rose lay back down again.

'Good girl.'

'So what tricks can Tiger do?' Michael asked Lucy.

Lucy pulled a strand of wool from her mum's knitting basket and waggled it in front of Tiger like a snake wriggling around the carpet. Tiger jumped off the armchair, stalked the wool and captured it with his paw.

Tail held high, he went over to Robert and then to Michael to allow them the honour of stroking him.

Tiger didn't need tricks to be admired.

megan rix

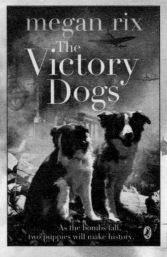

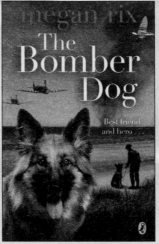

Find out more about Megan and her books at
www.meganrix.com

Bright and shiny and sizzling with fun stuff . . .

puffin.co.uk

WEB FUN

UNIQUE and exclusive digital content!
Podcasts, photos, Q&A, Day in the Life of, interviews
and much more, from Eoin Colfer, Cathy Cassidy,
Allan Ahlberg and Meg Rosoff to Lynley Dodd!

WEB NEWS

The **Puffin Blog** is packed with posts and photos from
Puffin HQ and special guest bloggers. You can also sign up
to our monthly newsletter **Puffin Beak Speak**

WEB CHAT

Discover something new EVERY month –
books, competitions and treats galore

WEBBED FEET

(Puffins have funny little feet and
brightly coloured beaks)

Point your mouse our way today!

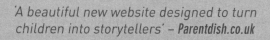

It all started with a Scarecrow.

Puffin is seventy years old.
Sounds ancient, doesn't it? But Puffin has never been
so lively. We're always on the lookout for the next big
idea, which is how it began all those years ago.

Penguin Books was a big idea from the mind of
a man called Allen Lane, who in 1935 invented
the quality paperback and changed the world.
**And from great Penguins, great Puffins grew,
changing the face of children's books forever.**

The first four Puffin Picture Books were hatched in 1940 and the
first Puffin story book featured a man with broomstick arms called
Worzel Gummidge. In 1967 Kaye Webb, Puffin Editor, started the
Puffin Club, promising to **'make children into readers'**.
She kept that promise and over 200,000 children became
devoted Puffineers through their quarterly instalments of
Puffin Post, which is now back for a new generation.

Many years from now, we hope you'll look back and
remember Puffin with a smile. **No matter what your age
or what you're into, there's a Puffin for everyone.**
The possibilities are endless, but one thing is for sure:
whether it's a picture book or a paperback, a sticker book
or a hardback, **if it's got that little Puffin
on it – it's bound to be good.**